Readers are saying...

"We stand on the shoulders of those who came before us. Naomi Krant, with her marvelous new novel, *Unexpected Legacy*, stands on the shoulders of the likes of Henry Roth, Mordechai Richler, Bernard Malamud and others who mined our ethnic, immigrant past to light our present and future ... Krant pulls you into a well-crafted inter-generational saga that bestows insights into ongoing issues of social turmoil and identity."

Marty Rosenberg
Journalist, *Kansas City Star*

"In *Unexpected Legacy*, Naomi Krant has spun an engrossing yarn that encompasses the hardships of Jewish-immigrant life circa 1909, and the altogether-different struggles of their descendants in the modern day. Krant skillfully weaves the two worlds into a connected whole."

Dan Freedman
Senior editor, *Moment Magazine*

"This touching novel about courage and persistence launches readers into Sol's story in New York City in 1909 and into his great grandchildren's story in 2009. A Jewish immigrant fleeing violent persecution in Poland, Sol must deal with prejudice in his new country as did each wave of immigrants coming to America. Details of tenement life and a mystery his descendants must solve make this novel a real page-turner. "

Marianne T. Rafter,
Author, *Dancing on the Brink of the World*

Unexpected Legacy

Unexpected Legacy

Naomi Krant

KAJAKI
PRESS

San Francisco

Table of Contents

Chapter 1

1909

"You can do it, Sol," Mendel said.

"Remember," Sol's sister Hanna cut in, "two cents for every cap you sell. We put forty in the suitcase."

"Forty!"

"Forty is nothing," Mendel said. "The tour boat holds two hundred and seventy-five people. You only have to sell twenty caps this morning and twenty this afternoon. There is an evening cruise, but I'm sure you'll sell everything before then. Soon you'll be selling seventy-five, a hundred caps a day. It's not hard. Look how colorful they are! People love them."

"Not hard for you, Mendel," Sol said, switching to Yiddish, the language of Eastern European Jews. "For me, it's not so easy to talk to strangers. In English!"

"Oh, stop whining," said Hanna. "I could do it."

Sol heard frustration in his sister's sharp tone. Hanna was always frustrated. She'd been one and a half when their mother died, and it seemed she'd never found the comfort she needed after that. Hanna had only recently been given to Mendel in marriage. She was seventeen, two years younger than Sol and half of her husband's age. Since her marriage, arranged by their stepmother, Matya, Hanna's bitterness had only increased.

Now Hanna and Mendel needed Sol to take over Mendel's job selling caps because Mendel was sick.

"That's not helping, Hanna," Mendel said. "He needs encouragement." He put his hand to his stomach and closed his eyes in pain. "Just try, Solly. I know you'll do fine."

At Manhattan's midtown pier, Sol stared at the gleaming white tour boat. It looked like the wedding cake in the window of Naftali's Bakery. The *Washington Irving* had three decks where passengers could sit or stand for the three-hour sightseeing cruise up the Hudson River. It was nothing like the *SS Nieuw Amsterdam*, the huge, black ship in which he had crossed the Atlantic Ocean to America four years earlier.

Each day during that week on the *SS Nieuw Amsterdam*, Sol had climbed four levels from the stinking bottom of the ship to stand in the wind, breathe fresh air, and feel amazed. He had never expected to be there, on his way to America to join his family. He'd been left behind in Poland to finish his education, but violence against Jews had overwhelmed his small village. Then one day, just when another pogrom was about to descend, his uncle had arrived at the gate of his school with a ticket.

Sol had certainly been glad to leave his small town, Volnavoda, with its population of old-fashioned Jews and Polish peasants. Most of all, he'd been glad to escape his strict religious school. Staring at the horizon from the deck of the *Nieuw Amsterdam*, Sol had dreamed of a new life in America where he could get a modern education.

Life in a new country had not been easy. He'd had to learn a new language. Jobs that hired immigrants hadn't paid enough. Everyone in the family had to contribute what they could towards the rent for their tiny apartment in the Lower East Side of New York City. On top of that, he no longer had a clear idea of his future. His step-mother had wanted him to work. She had been clear.

"He's fifteen. He should be saving money to start a marriage and a life," she'd said. She had made him feel like just another mouth to feed, another body that needed clothes and a place to sleep.

Seeing how the family struggled, Sol had been willing to work. But his father had had a different idea. Avram had insisted that he go to the public school to learn English and American ways, and for once he had overpowered his wife in a disagreement.

That nine months in classes with unruly young children was not the modern education Sol had hoped for.

After the school year at P.S. 147, he began work with a simple sewing job in the garment trade. Soon he moved on to saddling and unsaddling horses at a stable and delivery jobs. Before going to work for Mendel, he loaded and unloaded freight on the docks. He could read English, but this job would be his first in which speaking English was necessary. He didn't want to let his family down. He had to try.

ooo

Now standing next to where the tour boat was docked, he sighed. A man and a woman pushed past him and walked out along the pier. They gave tickets to a white-haired man at a gate.

Sol followed the couple and showed the ticket-taker Mendel's vendor pass.

"Kalinski's Caps?" the man read on the pass. "Where's Mendel?" By his musical way of speaking English and his green suspenders, Sol guessed that he was an Irishman.

"He...he's not well," Sol stammered. "I'll be working for him."

"Not well? Ach! Too bad! Always a cheerful fellow, Mendel. Always a good word! Is it serious? It isn't his heart, is it?"

Sol patted his stomach. "Ulcer," he said, pronouncing the word carefully.

"Ulcer! Who would have guessed?" The man shook his head sadly. Then he looked closely at Sol. "And what's your name?"

"Solomon—Solomon Lefkowitz."

"Jimmy O'Shea," the Irishman said, holding out a large hand. "Well, brighten up, young man! It's a lovely day and *everyone* has a good time on a Diamond Cruise."

Sol stretched his lips into a smile. But as he walked up the gangplank, he was so nervous that he felt seasick. And the boat wasn't even moving.

Three hours later, he was not even pretending to smile as he hauled his suitcase down to the dock. Two caps! He'd sold only two caps. His heart was as heavy as his case.

At first, as the boat pushed upstream along the Hudson River, Sol had called out the phrases Mendel taught him.

"Souvenirs! Beautiful caps! All colors!" he called, But people looked irritated and moved away from him. He thought it must be because his English was so bad.

When the ship reached the north end of its route, the small town of Yonkers, everyone rushed off to explore. When they returned, half an hour later, Sol was upset to see that many were wearing new caps. They must have bought them at a shop in town.

On that afternoon's cruise he tried hard to sell caps before the ship reached Yonkers. But he only sold four. He stayed on for the evening cruise, too, although it meant going without dinner. Selling on the evening cruise was even more difficult. Groups of tourists partied with bottles of liquor. Couples leaned against the rail with their heads together. Sol felt like an intruder. He felt lonely.

ooo

Mendel and Hanna were waiting up for him. Hanna had a plate of food keeping warm at the back of the coal stove.

"Well? How did you do?" Mendel asked. He knelt next to the suitcase and opened it. Caps spilled out.

"I said everything you told me to say!" Sol said. "They didn't pay attention."

"You didn't sell any?" Hanna asked.

"Eight," Sol said miserably.

"Eight! If Mendel came home with eight *left over* he would say he was a failure."

"*Sha*, Hanna," Mendel said, slowly standing. His hand covered his stomach.

"We should have hired Benny Bursov, like I told you," Hanna said. "Benny knows how to talk to people."

"Benny talks too much," Mendel said. "He forgets what he's supposed to be doing."

"I didn't forget," Sol said. "I tried. I don't know how to make people buy."

Hanna set the plate of food down hard in front of Sol. She had given him a whole chicken leg and a big slice of noodle pudding. Head down, Sol ate.

"Tomorrow I'll go with you, Sol. I'll teach you how to do it," Mendel said.

"You're not well enough to go," Hanna said. "That's why we hired him."

"I'll be fine," Mendel said.

ooo

"I know he'll be here. Can't you hold the ship for five minutes?" Sol begged Jimmy.

"It's not up to me," Jimmy said. "It's up to the captain. He runs the ship, you know."

Sol did know. On the third and fourth day of his journey across the Atlantic Ocean to America a woman and her two small daughters died of diphtheria. The woman's husband begged and cried for their bodies to be saved for a Jewish burial on land, but the captain threw them into the waves. Then he crossed their names off the ship's log.

"I'm going to tell the immigration officers those three stayed behind in Rotterdam," the captain said. "And you'd better back me up. If Immigration finds out there was diphtheria on this ship, you'll all be sent back to where you came from. All of you." When they reached New York, no one said a word about the deaths. Even the husband lied.

Jimmy waved Sol on board the *Washington Irving.*

Mendel didn't show up for the afternoon or evening cruises, either. When Sol went to Mendel's and Hanna's apartment, he found Mendel grey-faced, in bed, with Hanna by his side. No dinner waited on the back of the stove.

"How many?" Hanna asked.

"Twelve," Sol admitted.

Hanna burst into tears. "He needs a doctor! How are we going to pay?"

Sol bit his lip. There was nothing an immigrant needed more than good health.

"I'll be better tomorrow Hanna-le," Mendel said. But it was a week before he was on his feet again. Every night, Sol dragged himself up five flights of stairs to their tiny apartment. Hanna and Mendel met him, their faces more and more sullen. Sol even worked on Saturday, the Sabbath, which upset his stepmother.

On the following Monday, Mendel met him on the dock. His face was still grey and there were bags under his eyes.

"Mendel!" Jimmy reached out to clap Mendel on the shoulder, then stopped himself. "How are you? You don't look so good."

"No, I'm fine," Mendel said. He poked Sol to move ahead.

"Wait, now," Jimmy said. "Two of you? Your permit only allows one."

"Ah, Jimmy, I need to train him. Can't you bend the rule this once? He needs help."

Jimmy lifted his cap and ran his fingers through his hair. The cap was an old navy blue one, faded and dirty.

"Tch!" Mendel said. "That cap's a shame, Jimmy." In a flash, he snatched the suitcase from Sol's hand and pulled out a new, bright green cap. "Why don't you take this one? Green—matches your suspenders."

The Irishman's eyes lit up.

"Now, that's a bribe I'll take," he said. He nodded towards Sol. "You're right, he needs your help. It's OK, the boat won't fill up on a Monday morning. Good luck."

"I wish I'd thought of that," Sol said. He understood right away that passengers boarding the ship would notice the bright green hat and would want one.

Mendel patted him on the back. "You're a smart kid," he said. "You just need practice and some tips."

Sol sighed. What he needed was a salesman's personality. He headed for the side of the ship where he knew the passengers would gather for the best view of the city. As he neared the crowd, he cleared his throat.

"Souvenir caps!" he began. "Remember a beautiful day!" He put extra energy into his voice to show Mendel how hard he was trying. And because Mendel was listening, Sol listened to himself. "All the colors of happiness!" he half-sang.

Mendel grabbed his arm, whispering. "Stop! Stop! You sound like you are begging forgiveness for your sins on Yom Kippur!"

It was true. When had that tone of suffering and longing come into his call?

"Anyway," Mendel said, "that's the wrong way to begin. Here's what I do. Until we get to the north end of Manhattan Island, all you have to do is be friendly. Point out sights. Ask them if they've ever been on a cruise before. Just talk."

Mendel slapped a bright blue cap on his head and danced up to a family with three teenaged children. "What a day to be on the river!" he said. "I never get tired of this cruise. Is this your first time?"

The father smiled at Mendel's enthusiastic tone and said yes, it was. The middle child, a boy of about fourteen, nudged his father. "Pa, can you buy us caps?" he asked.

"That was too easy," Mendel said to Sol afterward. "Don't expect that to happen very often!"

The boat's motors started with a roar. Smoke poured out of two of the three stacks. Trembling with power, the *Washington Irving* backed away from the pier. Mendel hardly glanced at the view of the city. But he seemed to know exactly which buildings they were passing, and he was able to point them out to the people he was talking with. He climbed from deck to deck, weaving through the crowds, greeting tourists as if they were old friends. Most people returned Mendel's hellos and answered his smiles with their smiles.

Only once did Mendel pause, stepping through a door into a stairwell. Out of sight of any tourists, he leaned against the metal wall with his eyes closed. "Just need a minute," he whispered. His face was pale.

When he stepped back out into the sun a minute later, his smile was sunny, too.

"Why don't you give it a try?" he said, handing Sol the suitcase.

Sol had been expecting that, but his teeth clamped together, and his throat tightened.

His eyes fell on a young woman standing alone at the rail. She looked a little like his sister, Hanna. One person was easier to speak to than a whole group.

"Very nice day to be out on the river, don't you think?" he asked her.

She jumped and turned startled eyes on him. "I... Excuse me...." She whispered, backing away.

Mendel's hand clamped down on Sol's shoulder.

"What are you thinking?" Mendel hissed in his ear. "Nice girls don't talk to men they don't know! Especially nice American girls to *greenhorns* like us."

"Sorry, sorry!" Sol said, as much to Mendel as to the young woman. She had already joined a well-dressed young man and was speaking to him with her back turned to Sol. The young man looked hard at Sol and Mendel, then shrugged.

Sol felt as though he was back in school at the Great Synagogue in his Polish village and he had given the wrong answer in front of the whole class.

"No," he told himself firmly. "I'm not in Poland. I'm in America. I can do this. I have to do this."

Taking a deep breath, he pulled a bright yellow cap down over his dark hair and approached a family with two small children.

"Isn't this a beautiful day for a cruise?" he asked the father.

Chapter 2
2009

One hundred years later, a young woman named Miri Perelman climbed the dirty marble steps from the Essex Street subway station. This was the old Lower East Side of New York City—the landing place for wave after wave of new immigrants. According to Miri's mother, that included Miri's own great-grandfather, Solomon Lefkowitz, who had arrived in the United States just over a hundred years before.

The smell of McDonald's fries drifted on the hot July air. She pulled her phone out of the front pocket of her jeans and stopped, to shade it from the sun. Someone ran into her from behind.

She jumped aside with a little scream. Her heart raced.

But it wasn't an attack. It was just a young man who must have been following her too closely. He had acorn-brown skin, light blue hair, and a gold stud in the shape of a snake on his nose. A faint Caribbean beat leaked from his wireless headphones. He passed her and walked on without even a sideways glance. His attitude said *This is my neighborhood now.*

"Fine," Miri murmured. She felt no particular connection to the place. And her scream had just been a leftover from the now-ended relationship with her ex-boyfriend, Chuck, whose habit of giving her shoves when she didn't agree with him had accelerated to the point of danger.

Her phone said twelve forty-five, fifteen minutes early for her one-o'clock lunch date with her cousin Dalia. She turned the corner and walked west along Delancey Street. But before she'd walked a single block, a Japanese screen in the window of an antiques store caught her eye.

Mid-Edo Period, she thought. That would make it two hundred years old. She knew all about the painting technique. The artist had used a brush thinned to a single hair to paint the details of the trees and birds on the gold background. It was exquisite.

Miri stepped closer. A price tag on a string was carefully turned so she couldn't read it from outside the store. She sighed. Never mind. Her pay from the art gallery where she worked wasn't even enough to cover her rent, food, and student loan payments. She'd had to ask her father for money. It was humiliating.

ooo

At the upscale Brazilian restaurant, she ordered a slushy limeade from the bar. A couple was just leaving an outside table as she finished paying. Perfect. Miri sank into a chair.

The first icy mouthful of her drink sent a sharp pain to her head just as her phone buzzed. Eyes squeezed shut, she answered.

"On your way?" she asked, assuming it was Dalia calling.

There was a silence on the other end.

"Hello?" she tried. "Who is this?"

"Seth."

Seth? The man's voice was a little rough, abrupt. Her finger had almost touched the red end-call icon when he spoke again.

"Seth Lefkowitz. Your cousin. From Battle Hill."

"Seth?"

An image flashed through Miri's mind: a child's sparkling blue eyes. It was at a family wedding reception. She and a mischievous boy with a mop of curly orange hair were under a table. She must have been four, he six. Surrounding them were men's legs in dark trousers and women's skirts billowing over their evening sandals. She and the boy tickled the women's feet, then scrambled away, giggling, each trying to outdo the other—until he went too far. He pulled a corner of the white tablecloth. After-dinner drinks and coffees toppled into laps. Feet jerked; adults screamed. The gleam in the boy's eyes turned to panic. Arms extended into their cave and pulled them out. His parents left hastily, dragging him along.

"Wow!" Miri said into the phone. "How many years has it been? How are you?"

"Yeah, fine," he said flatly.

The mischievous little boy vanished from Miri's imagination like a candle being blown out.

"Hey," he went right on, "I heard you know a lot about art. Can we meet? I have something I need to show you."

"Uh…art?"

Now Miri remembered two reasons why she hadn't seen this cousin since they were small. First, his family had moved to Seattle years ago. And second, Seth had problems.

Her mom had told her that much on the phone a few months earlier. One of his problems was that his mother, Miri's aunt, had died when Seth was nine. He'd been raised by his father. But he had a more immediate problem of some sort. It had caused him to leave the West Coast and move back to Battle Hill, a suburb north of New York City. Miri's aunt hadn't explained what the recent problem was.

"Yeah, like, a drawing," Seth was saying. "Where are you? I'm at your apartment, but you're not home."

"You're at my apartment?" Miri told herself to keep calm. There wasn't any reason to be alarmed.

"Yeah. Can we meet? I took today off work."

"Today? I'm grabbing lunch right now and I have to get back to the gallery."

"This would only take a minute. I just need to know if it's worth anything or not."

That was so ridiculous that Miri almost snorted. Art appraisal—estimating the value of a piece of art—was complicated! It took years of experience to be any good at it. She now had the necessary university degrees, but she was only an intern at the gallery, working for barely more than minimum wage. No matter what track she decided to follow—appraiser, curator for a big gallery, or something different—she had a long climb in the art world before her opinion was worth even two cents.

"Bring it to MIMA," she said and took a tiny sip of her drink.

"Who's that?"

"That's where I work. Manhattan Institute of Modern Art. Someone there will help you."

"Nnn, I can't do that. Listen, can I come by wherever you are when you're finished with lunch?"

No, Miri almost said. But at that moment, she spotted Dalia walking towards the restaurant, and she had another idea. She could use Dalia's help with this.

"Actually," she said, "I'm having lunch with our cousin Dalia. Why don't you join us?"

"Dalia? Rayna's daughter? Is she the one who's a lawyer?"

"Uh-huh."

"That's not going to work." he mumbled. And hung up.

"Hello, there," Dalia greeted her. "That's a phone you're glaring at, not a dead cockroach. Was that a call from someone threatening you about your credit card debt?"

Dalia's dark, straight hair was pulled back into a bun, showing off large silver and turquoise earrings. A silk dress printed with bright flowers floated around her. She settled into the chair opposite Miri and slid the strap of one high-heeled sandal off the back of her foot with a sigh.

Miri assumed it was Dalia's husband, Josh, who paid for Dalia's expensive clothes and jewelry. Dalia worked for a small, socially-conscious law firm that took a lot of legal aid cases. Josh, whom she'd married in law school, worked for one of New York's large law firms and probably made three times her salary.

"That was our cousin, Seth," Miri said.

"Oh, I've heard stories about *him*," Dalia said.

"What?"

"The kind of thing I hear about my clients all the time," Dalia said. "A little shoplifting as a kid. Teen-aged anxiety. Parents took him to a psychiatrist, and he abused the pills—a Xanax-type drug. Addictive. Seth got caught buying them on the street and got kicked out of university after only one term. Bad luck, really."

"Mom told me he'd moved back to Battle Hill, but she didn't say why."

"Mm-hm. Moved to get a fresh start, after he got off parole."

"Parole? For what?"

"For buying the Xanax. I looked up the record when I heard about it from my mom. He only got one week in jail, six months of parole. That's fairly light. Uncle Ira must have gotten him a good lawyer."

"Oh." Now Miri really wished that Seth had agreed to meet with the two of them. She was sure he'd call her again and she really didn't want to deal with him by herself.

Dalia raised an eyebrow. "Did he call you just to say hello? I tried calling him when I heard he'd moved here, but he wouldn't talk to me."

"I guess he doesn't like lawyers." Miri repeated her conversation with Seth.

"Hmm," Dalia said. "So, he thinks this drawing is valuable, but he won't talk to an art dealer, and he doesn't want a lawyer involved. Sounds fishy. Where did he get this piece of art? This calls for the kind of tactic we use at work to get someone to tell the truth." She chewed on her bottom lip and squinted at the sky. "OK, I have a plan," she said.

Seth almost didn't answer when Miri called him back. At the last second, he growled, "'Lo."

She spoke quickly so he wouldn't hear her nervousness. "Seth? Listen, Dalia got here; she's in the restroom. She's on a big case and she has to be back to her office by one-thirty. So come by after that and I'll look at the drawing."

He considered this.

"I can't pay you," he said.

"I know. It's just a…a family favor."

"I dunno. You might not know about this thing," he muttered. Clearly, he was having second thoughts.

"Is it contemporary, this drawing?"

"Define contemporary."

"Twentieth or twenty-first century?"

"Yeah, I think so," he said.

"I'd know about it." She hoped he wouldn't hear that she was bluffing.

He grunted agreement.

Miri explained where she was. "Call me when you get to Essex Street," she added.

"Call you? Why?"

"So I know you're really coming," she said as firmly as she could. She didn't want to be taken by surprise.

"Hmh!" he said, and hung up again.

"Sounds like he bought it," Dalia said.

Miri ran her fingers through her curls and let out a long breath.

Just then, a waitress appeared with menus. "We're in a hurry," Dalia told her. They both ordered salads. "And an iced tea for me," Dalia added, a shadow of regret in her voice.

When the waitress had left, she reached for Miri's drink, sniffed it, and took a tiny sip. "Plain limeade?"

"Yup."

If Dalia was disappointed, she hid it. "How's your job, going, by the way?" she asked.

"Internships suck," Miri said. "Especially if your boss is Bret."

"I know," Dalia said. "You do all the dumb and dirty work, and the pay is mostly the shiny reference letter he's going to write for you. Just keep in mind how very, very useful a great reference from Bret will be."

Dalia was seven years older than Miri and liked to play the big sister. She always asked about Miri's life and always had advice. She hardly ever said anything about herself.

OOO

The restaurant was starting to clear out after the lunch rush. Miri and Dalia both put their phones on the table so they could keep track of the time.

"I said to come after one-thirty. He couldn't get here any sooner, anyway," Miri said.

Still, when a table nearby emptied at one-twenty, Dalia pushed her chair back and stood up.

"I'm going to grab that," she said. She gathered her plate and silverware. "I'll have my eye on you. Remember: get facts." She carried everything to the empty table and chose a seat where she could see Miri's face. The next moment, she was smiling at a small boy who was wriggling in his chair. The child immediately got down and ran over to her. This was predictable; Dalia was a magnet for small children.

Miri toyed with her salad. Dalia obviously had no worries about her plan. But she hadn't talked with Seth. Miri began replaying the phone conversation in her mind. The more she thought about how rough Seth sounded and what Dalia had told her about him, the more anxious she felt. She was just thinking of getting up and leaving, blowing the whole thing off, when she spotted him—she was sure it was him—coming down the street.

Of course he hadn't called.

The man striding towards her was wide-shouldered and lean. His hair was a mop of auburn curls held off his face by a black sports visor. His eyebrows were dark and heavy and he had an unusual beard, shaved into two sections with his bare chin exposed in the middle. A brown paper bag from a Foodtown Supermarket dangled from one hand.

He didn't pause for even a second to sweep his eyes over the customers. He walked straight to Miri, noisily pulled back the chair across from her, and sat.

"Seth," he stated.

Chapter 3
1909

The first week after Mendel's lesson on how to sell caps, Sol did a little better. Most days, he sold between twelve and eighteen. One lucky day, he sold twenty-five and made fifty cents for himself. But he needed more money than that. Hanna and Mendel needed more money, too. Instead of selling more, though, he began to sell fewer. The next week, he sold twelve te first day, ten the next.

"What's the trouble, Sol?" Mendel asked. He was not unkind.

"Just a bad day," Sol said. "Tomorrow will be better again."

Mendel sighed. "It will have to be," he said. "We're buying groceries on credit now. I need a salesman who will bring in money right away. If you don't sell more caps than this...." He didn't finish his sentence, but Sol knew what Mendel meant: *I'll have to hire someone else.*

"His trouble is he's too serious," Hanna said. She made a dramatically long face. "I don't think he knows how to laugh."

"I can laugh." Sol said. He smiled as brightly as he could.

"Yes, you have nice teeth," Hanna said. "With that smile, you could probably sell caps to all the ladies on the boat. But laugh? No. You don't have a light spirit, Sol."

ooo

It was true. At his yeshiva, the religious high school at the Great Synagogue of Volnavoda, Rabbi Yehudah told him many times to study less, have more fun. "Why don't you throw sticks for the dog?" he asked. The old man's back was so bent that the front of his black robe scraped the ground; he often tripped on it. His long grey beard was tipped with ink where it smeared across the letters that he wrote to raise money for the school. "Climb a tree," he continued. "Go to the henhouse and find an egg. Try to walk with the egg balanced on your nose."

All the rabbis delighted in suggesting mystical or amazing activities that might show evidence of God's presence, or at least give some joy.

Sol tipped his head to one side and squinted. "It would fall off and break."

The rabbi waved him away. "Bah!" he said, "You should laugh more, Solomon. There is too much trouble in the world already. Soothing bruised souls is a great *mitzvah* and part of a rabbi's job. And for that, a sense of humor is very helpful."

The trouble was that Sol didn't want to be a rabbi.

His father, Avram, owned a fabric shop in the Jewish town of Volnavoda. The town was in the part of the Russian Pale of Settlement that had originally been part of the First Polish Republic [a]. Avram was also employed as one of the many estate managers by the Polish nobleman who owned the town. Avram wasn't the most important manager, but his position gave him some importance in town and a house on the nicest street. It also gave him enough money to keep his oldest son in school at the Great Synagogue, the only high school that Jews could attend.

But finishing school meant Sol would be eligible to become a rabbi—and the very idea filled him with dread. How could he lead people toward a God he had trouble understanding himself? How could he help them solve moral problems that made no sense to him? Also, studying the six hundred and thirteen religious commandments in ancient Jewish texts bored him to death. The commandments did not answer any of the questions he had about life. It took all his strength to spend the necessary hours at his studies. He only did it so he would not bring shame on his family and himself.

What interested him were modern books on science, in particular, the new science of psychology. He smuggled those books into the dormitory and read them in secret. They were his private window into a larger world. He had no idea how he would enter it.

The life he really wanted was to work in a laboratory. He dreamed of the experiments he would carry out as he studied the mysteries of the human brain. But he would need a university degree for that, and the few Jews who were admitted into Russian universities came from rich families in Moscow, families with friends in the nobility. No, the life he wanted was impossible for him in Russian Poland.

Here in America, there was hope. Hope was the immigrant's dinner and the blanket that kept him warm at night. In America, every morning could bring something new, something he had never imagined.

Although, to tell the truth, selling souvenir caps on the Washington Irving was as boring as his studies at the yeshiva had been. No, it wasn't just boring—Sol was coming to dread it. Hanna was right: light conversation was difficult for him, and with strangers it was worse.

But his father and stepmother were feeding him, giving him a place to sleep, even if it was on the couch. The months he'd spent in the neighborhood public school had delayed him from earning money, but now he needed to contribute to the family. So he would try harder. He knew what he had to do. He had to speak light and friendly English, to show people that Kalinski's caps went with smiles and a happy day.

The next morning, he left his stepmother's black tea for his younger half-brothers and spent the profit of one hat on a cup of bitter coffee-house coffee, sweetened with sugar. Coffee was one of the most wonderful things about America. In Poland, they had a drink called coffee, but it was made from chicory. Real coffee was entirely different, he'd discovered. It raised his energy. It brightened his spirits. He sold four caps before the ship even left the dock. And then two more before it passed 42nd Street. A great start!

After that, there was a lull. But Sol knew what to do.

"Best price on the best-made caps!" he called, in a caffeine-bright voice. "Yellow! Red! Beautiful blue! Lowest price you'll find!" He intended this message to pay off after the stop at Yonkers. Usually he sold most of his caps on the return trip and today he would sell a lot. Today his bad luck was over.

"Lowest price, highest quality!" he called. No one responded. They were all standing at the rail, taking in the view of New York's tall buildings on one side and New Jersey's tree-covered hills on the other. He even chatted with a few people about how fine the day was, careful to speak only to families with kids. No one asked to buy a cap. That was OK. When they saw what was on sale at the Yonkers General Store, they would remember him.

At Yonkers, Sol got off with most of the passengers and bought a second cup of coffee at a stand on the dock. He loaded it with even more sugar than he'd put in his first cup.

After a short walk, he found himself singing. Singing! It was a song he'd heard coming from a bar on Essex Street, on his way home from the coffee house when he'd tagged along with his classmates from English class. That was before he worked for Mendel. Now he had no time for friends.

"Come away with me, Lucille, in my merry Oldsmobile...." he sang. The cheerful tune made him smile, and at the same time it made him sad. How he missed conversations with his friends!

When Sol returned to the boat, the passengers were already filing on board. Jimmy waved him past. He climbed the stairs two at a time, straight up to the third deck. There was no shade at all up there, and the passengers were sure to want caps.

At the top of the stairs, a middle-aged man in a fashionable suit, high collar, and tie, stood at the rail with a younger woman. In contrast to the man's proper appearance, the woman wore a daringly short skirt, well above her ankles, and a plain white shirt. Light brown curls had sprung loose from her high puff of hair. She raised a graceful hand to smooth it.

But it was the book in the man's hand that really caught Sol's attention. The words on its spine gleamed gold in the sunlight. The title was in German, which he could not read, but below it was the author's name.

"Sigmund Freud!" he exclaimed.

The man and the young woman turned. The woman's thinned and arched eyebrows gave her a questioning expression that the man did not have. But their hazel eyes and wide mouths were so similar that Sol realized they must be father and daughter.

"You're interested in Freud?" the father asked.

The young people at the Essex Street coffee house spoke excitedly of Freud. Back in Volnavoda, Sol had bought second-hand books by Russian and German psychologists. Those books explained how the nervous system worked — how the mind received information from the five senses and then gave directions to the body. That was certainly fascinating. But the Austrian Freud was different. Freud told how the mind *thought* — how it imagined, how it cared, what it knew about itself, and what it hid from itself.

"I have heard a lot about him," Sol said. He did not add that Freud's books were not yet translated into Yiddish or any language he could read.

The daughter's eyes searched Sol, interested. The man cocked his head, listening to Sol's accent. "I suppose you don't read German," he said.

Sol flushed. "No, only Polish and Russian. And now I study English." He could have said that he read Hebrew and Yiddish, too, but after all, what was written in those languages besides religious books and his mother's newspaper, *The Jewish Daily Forward*?

"You study at the Educational Alliance?"

"Yes." Sol didn't want to talk about his current English class. "Please," he said, "is it true that Freud tells what dreams mean?"

The daughter's eyebrow quirked. The father's mouth twisted into a small smile.

"In a way," he said. Was his tone of voice condescending? Sol wasn't sure.

Just then, the boat's horn gave a long blast. Propellers churned the water. Trembling with effort, the boat backed slowly away from the dock. It was too noisy for conversation for almost a full minute, but finally the man continued.

"Freud tells how the mind expresses its hidden thoughts in dreams."

Hidden thoughts! From the smiles and winks between the young men at the coffee house, Sol had gathered that Freud's ideas included a lot about sex. This was a subject in which Sol had no experience, but intense interest.

Perhaps the man saw that interest on Sol's face.

"I'm sure a nice yeshiva boy like you would not have had the opportunity under the rabbis to study Freud," he said. This time, the man's belittling tone was clear.

"Papa!" the daughter said. "You should listen to yourself!"

"Oh," the man said, raising one hand in a negative gesture. "I didn't mean to criticize *you*. It's the rabbis in those Russian schools, their mysticism, their anti-science attitude! I wish I could say that you'll find a better education at the Educational Alliance. As a member of the Jewish community, I support it, but some of the reports I hear don't please me."

This man was a Jew? Sol was amazed. He didn't look or speak like any Jew that Sol knew. But at the same time, the man's opinions about the rabbis back in Volnavoda were exactly the same as Sol's opinions. Anti-science? Definitely! They were straight from the Middle Ages.

"Shouldn't we introduce ourselves?" the daughter prompted.

"Of course, of course," her father said. "I'm Herbert Koestlic. and this is my daughter, Rose." He held out a hand.

"Solomon Lefkowitz," Sol said, shaking the man's hand. He shook the hand Rose offered, too. It was very smooth and soft; the nails were clean little ovals. He could feel himself blushing. Rose, however, behaved as if shaking hands with young men was completely ordinary.

"Pleased to meet you, Mr. Lefkowitz," she said. The warmth in her voice left no doubt that she was sincere.

To cover his awkwardness, Sol began to chatter about the German psychologists he remembered.

"Ah, yes, Wundt," Mr. Koestlic said dismissively.

"But how is Freud different?" Sol asked.

"Wundt measured. He measured small things like how many numbers a person can remember. Freud considers the whole person. He looks at social behavior, sexual urges, and traumatic experiences. Everything."

Sol blinked. His own father talked freely about politics and union organizing. But sexuality and traumatic experiences? In front of his daughter, Hanna? Never.

He glanced at Rose to see her reaction.

She smiled. "I've read the book," she said. Sol found her smile enchanting. And energizing. Questions began to explode in his brain and into speech.

Mr. Koestlic glanced pointedly at Sol's suitcase of caps. "Are you sure you have time?" he asked.

"Oh, yes!"

"Very well," Mr. Koestlic said. He flipped open the thick book and began to describe what was inside. Sol listened; he asked; he asked as many questions as he wanted to.

Mr. Koestlic's eyes wandered several times from the book to Sol's suitcase. But Sol was blind to this hint. It was as if an enormous bowl of ice cream—something he had only tasted twice in his life—had been placed before him. He wanted to finish every spoonful of it.

Suddenly, the steady vibration of the ship's motors changed, slowed. A shadow fell across the upper deck. Sol glanced around. The tall buildings of downtown New York City blocked the morning sun. They were minutes from the dock. The trip was over, and he hadn't sold a single cap.

An immense weight fell on his heart. Perhaps a sound came from his throat, but his tongue was frozen.

The Koestlics' eyes were on him. Mr. Koestlic had stopped speaking. Slowly, he closed the book of Freud's writings. Rose reached a hand toward Sol.

"Are you all right, Mr. Lefkowitz?" she asked.

"I....Yes. Yes. Will you excuse me, please? Thank you," Sol managed to say. Then, "Thank you for talking with me. Thank you."

He fled down the stairs.

Passengers were already crowded at the place where the gangplank would be extended. Sol pushed to the front.

"Ma! The cap seller!" a nearby child called out.

"Shh! You don't need a cap now. We're almost back at the dock," a woman answered.

What had he done? Sol thought. He'd failed, failed when he had success firmly in his hands! And he hardly knew how it had happened. He bowed his head, held his breath, and stared at the feet of the people around him. Their shoes were shined. New. His were falling apart, the broken laces knotted together.

By keeping his body rigid, his thoughts on shoes, he kept himself from despair. But the moment his beat-up shoes stepped onto the pier, it was as though the day turned to night. The sun itself could not penetrate the gloom that closed in on him.

He began to walk in no particular direction.

Why had he taken this job? The job he'd had before this one was in a warehouse next to the docks. He'd been part of a crew stacking crates that were brought off the big ships and then unstacking them and loading them onto carts and trucks. It was heavy work. At first, he wasn't up to it. The other men on the crew made fun of him: Greenhorn! Schoolboy! *Nebbish!* He'd stuck with it, though. The first week, his body hurt all the time. But gradually he began to feel stronger, and the work got easier. After only two months, though, all the workers on the waterfront went on strike. Sol wanted to carry a sign on the dock, and Avram would have agreed, but his stepmother Matya was against it. She was against any anti-establishment action. She said the shipping company would send thugs to beat up the strikers, and sure enough, they did. The strike went on and on, and because Sol had not worked long enough to join the union, he received no strike pay.

So, when Mendel offered him the job selling caps and Sol's father had urged him to help out Hanna and Mendel, Sol said yes. He'd almost made it past the hard beginning… He'd almost gotten to the point when it got easier. But now….

His eyes fell on a clock in the window of a barber shop. One-thirty-five! The afternoon sailing was at two o'clock! He looked around. Where was he? Somewhere way uptown. He turned and began to jog south, his suitcase banging against his leg.

The departing blast of the *Washington Irving's* horn sounded when Sol was still four blocks from the dock. He started to run, but it was no use. Turning the corner, he saw the widening strip of green water between the boat and the pier. He was too late.

ooo

Instead of taking the bus, Sol walked the mile and a half across town to Mendel's apartment. By the time he arrived, his mind had settled into an uncomfortable decision.

Hanna opened the door.

"Sol? What are you doing here?"

"Can you get Mendel, please?"

Hanna looked frightened. When she turned towards the bedroom, Sol saw a young, blond woman he did not know sitting on the couch. Their eyes met; he looked away quickly.

"Solly?" Mendel came out of the bedroom door, his hand to his stomach. "What happened?"

"I'm sorry." Sol kept his voice low because of the blond woman. "I...I messed up. I talked to a customer too long on the morning run and then....and then I missed the afternoon boat. I'm sorry, Mendel. I feel terrible."

He had decided that he would not quit. But he knew what was coming.

Mendel closed his eyes and leaned against the door.

"Sol," he said, "I have no choice. I have to fire you."

ooo

At the dinner table, Avram groaned when Sol admitted that he'd lost his job.

"Ach! I hoped it would work out. You needed a job. Mendel needed help." He shook his head.

Sol's half-brothers Bennie and Bernie, aged eleven and nine, stared at him with uneasy fascination as if he were a dead rat.

"What'd you do?" Bennie asked.

"Bennie," Avram said. "Be kind to your brother."

"I didn't sell enough caps." Sol said, feeling miserable.

"Not surprising," Bennie said.

"Bennie!"

"Well, he's not a salesman, is he?" Bennie said. "He's a teacher." He looked directly into Sol's eyes. "He can really explain stuff…if you ask him. *Selling* is different."

The whole family stared at Bennie. A tense knot just below Sol's breastbone loosened. His eyes prickled.

"*Nu, a kindersher saichel!*" Avram said. *A child's wisdom.*

Sol wanted to tell Bennie that sometimes you had to learn to do things that didn't come naturally, but he couldn't get the words out.

"Bennie is right," Avram said. "It's a shame for Mendel and Hanna's sake. But now at least you know: that kind of job isn't for you. So you'll try something else and do much better. I lost a couple of jobs, too, when we first got here. You keep trying, that's all."

"Well, we hope it's for the best," Matya said, clearly not believing her own words.

Chapter 4

2009

Up close, Seth looked seedy. His faded blue t-shirt was frayed at the neck. He'd obviously cut his own hair: the pile of auburn curls above the black visor was higher on one side than the other. Between his extra-long sideburns there was a shaving cut on his small, pointed chin.

He had pulled his chair well back from the table so he could display the Foodtown shopping bag prominently in his lap.

"How did you spot me?" Miri blurted. If she'd been the one approaching, she would never have picked him. This awkward man was nothing like the impish boy she remembered.

He smiled briefly. "You were the only one watching for me." In person, his voice was less growly than over the phone.

"The last I remember of you, we were under the table at someone's wedding. Was it Uncle David?"

"I think so. Yeah, David," he said shortly. Obviously, he didn't want to spend time remembering the past. He jiggled one leg, making the paper bag bounce.

Miri ignored his body language. As Dalia had charged, she needed to get more facts before moving on to whatever was in the bag.

"So, what are you doing in Battle Hill?" she asked.

"Construction."

Miri nodded. "I visited Great Aunt Rina in Battle Hill when I first came to New York. I saw a lot of construction going on downtown."

Seth's reply was drowned out by a large truck rattling by.

"What?"

"…doing demo right now," he muttered.

"Oh. Tearing down a building, you mean?"

"Nnh, a little old house." His expression lightened and he gave the brown paper bag in his lap a big bump with one thigh. "That's where I found this."

"Oh? You *found* it?"

Seth licked his lips and looked around. Tipping his chair back, he raised a hand to catch the attention of a waitress, who was carrying an overloaded tray.

"Can I get a water, here?" he asked loudly. Miri thought he only did that to avoid her question.

The waitress pressed her lips together without bothering to answer.

Seth shifted restlessly in his chair. He was anxious, Miri realized—more anxious than she was. On second thought, maybe he wanted the water to calm his nerves. She felt the beginning of sympathy: so they were both nervous.

He cleared his throat. "What do you do at that gallery you work at, anyway?"

"I'm an intern. I do whatever. Pack art, unpack art, hang it, clean it, type lists for the sales notebook, do research to see if it's authentic, …"

"Authentic? So, you can tell if something's real or fake? Can you tell what it's worth?"

Miri almost laughed. "No one knows what art is worth until it sells," she said, "especially something by an unknown artist. I can't tell you anything for certain. But go ahead, show me what you have."

Seth twitched his mouth to one side and opened the bag. He pulled out a dusty wooden frame. It held a charcoal drawing on cream-colored paper, framed and covered with glass. He handed it to her across the table.

Even before her brain completely registered what she was seeing, Miri's heart gave an enormous thump. The sensuous lines and shapes were unmistakable.

Seth was watching her face. "It's good, isn't it?" he said softly.

She had lost her words. It couldn't be true. And yet, all of her training said it was.

"*Tell me,*" Seth said.

Miri ran a finger over the crackled lacquer finish of the frame. Dalia's instruction came back to her. She raised her eyes from the drawing. "First, *you* tell *me*—am I looking at a stolen object?"

"What? No!"

"Then where did you get this?"

"I didn't steal it."

"Where?" she demanded. Her professional instinct had taken control.

"I told you. I found it at the house I'm working on." Then his face changed. "OK, never mind! Forget it." He reached for the art.

Instantly, Miri stood and stepped backward, her arms cradling the drawing. Her chair clattered to the sidewalk behind her. People turned their heads. Out of the corner of her eye, she saw that Dalia had swung around to face them. Holding her phone at lap level, she was calmly videoing.

Seth rose and came halfway around the table. Miri stepped sideways, keeping the table between them.

"Everyone's taking your picture!" she hissed.

That worked. He stepped back and sank into his chair, glancing around the outdoor tables. She used the moment to bring her own phone out of her pocket, clutching the framed drawing against her body with one arm.

"Everything okay here?" a male voice asked. A waiter in a black t-shirt and apron stood beside her.

"Yes. We're fine," Miri said.

He picked up her chair.

"Thanks," she said.

The waiter stood for a moment assessing Seth, who took a deep breath and exhaled through his nose.

"Fine," he said. "No problem." The waiter nodded and left.

Miri sat, still clutching the drawing. "OK, what I *think* this is, is an early drawing by Georgia O'Keeffe."

Seth's eyes lit up. "She's famous," he said.

"You could say that," Miri said dryly . "She's only one of the most famous artists of the twentieth century."

Already, in the back of her mind, a fantasy was beginning to unwind. This would be big news in the art world. It would be reported in the press, broadcast on social media — she could spread it all over her Instagram page. Her name would forever be linked with it. This would look far stronger on her resumé than a whole year of being a lowly intern in Bret's gallery. Her father would have to eat crow.

"Like, how much is it worth?"

"Well, one of O'Keeffe's most famous oil paintings sold for forty-four million just a few years ago. But for a little charcoal drawing like this…I don't know. If I'm right and it's really an O'Keeffe, I'd guess somewhere between a quarter of a million and half a million." She laid the frame down carefully on the tablecloth and holding her camera over it, shot a burst of photos.

Seth was frozen, stunned by what she'd said. "Half a million?" he breathed. "Whoa!"

"Maybe," Miri stressed. *You could be wrong*, she told herself. Less than ten years ago, art experts had been fooled by a cache of newly discovered O'Keeffe works that turned out to be fake. But her gut feeling said that she was right.

It took a good ten seconds more for Seth's eyes to snap into focus on her phone. "Hey! What are you doing?" Reaching across the table, he succeeded in snatching up the framed drawing. "Delete those photos! Family favor — ha! I might have known you couldn't be trusted!"

"No, you *can* trust me," she said. "The reason I want photos is because I need to research this. I think this is an unknown O'Keeffe. That means it might be an important discovery!" She paused and stared at him to make sure he understood.

"Unknown….Would that make it worth even more?" he asked, missing her point entirely.

"It could, yes," she admitted. "Maybe a lot more," she added. Her point had been that it would be important in the art world.

He looked at Miri's phone, clearly undecided. But apparently, the possibility of more money tipped the balance. He nodded.

Miri felt Dalia sending her a mental message: Get facts!

"You still haven't told me exactly where you got this," she said.

"Yeah, I did. I found it."

"You'll have to say more than that."

"No. I've already told you enough." His eyes checked her out and he nodded. "You'll look into it," he said. Then, stiffly, "Thanks."

Standing up, he stuffed the frame into the bag and tucked the package under his arm.

Miri winced. She wanted to tell him how to handle a precious piece of art. Carrying it in a paper bag was crazy! It would be much safer if he left it with her.

"Wait…. Let's talk some more," she almost begged. But he wasn't going to wait.

"I'll call you tomorrow after work," he said. Turning, he almost collided with the waitress, who was just arriving with his glass of water. He stepped smoothly around her and strode off down the sidewalk. Miri kept her eyes on his retreating back. The chance of a lifetime was crushed against his side. Her anxious thoughts must have reached him, because after ten yards, he halted and carefully removed the bag from under his arm. Walking on, he held it against his chest with both arms.

Miri blew out a long breath.

"You're welcome," she muttered.

Chapter 5

1909

Sol had come early to get a seat in his English class at the Educational Alliance, a community center for immigrants. By the time class started, men sat on the floor in front of the desks and stood along the back wall of the classroom. The windows were pushed wide open, but the weak breeze did not dry the sweat that trickled down the sides of Sol's face. The heavy air smelled of working men's bodies.

At least he went to school with adults now. That first school year in the public elementary school where his father had sent him had been terrible. In Poland, he'd been one of the best students in his high school; in America, he'd had to begin again, in the first grade. He'd stuffed his body into a tiny desk chair, and he'd written the English alphabet on paper with lines three centimeters apart. The Irish and Italian kids made fun of him and of the other over-age boys in the class. They called him names like *Yid* and *sheeny*. They put horse droppings on his chair and insects in his lunch. The other over-age kids in the class put a stop to this treatment right away. They hit the little pests out on the playground, when the teachers weren't looking. But Sol didn't want to do that, so all the persecution was focused on him. Every six or eight weeks, when he'd mastered the skills in a grade, he moved up to a higher level, and each time, he hoped he was escaping to a nicer group of kids. But it never made any difference. Kids on the Lower East Side were rough.

A half-folded note lay on Teacher Weiss's desk. The class had already finished writing practice, but Teacher Weiss stopped the student helpers from collecting the slates and chalk. These signs, Sol recognized.

"All right, class," Teacher Weiss said, unfolding the note. "Pick up your slates. We will finish tonight with a little extra writing practice." The curve of his usual smile had become a straight line. "Number one," he dictated. "Americans respect a man dressed in fresh, clean clothing."

The class sighed. Chalk clicked and squeaked on small slates.

Teacher Weiss wrote the sentence on the blackboard so the students could check their spelling.

"Number two," he read. He hesitated, one eyebrow raised, before he continued. "The American gentleman takes great care with his toilet."

There was a moment of silence.

Then a roar of laughter exploded. Teacher Weiss held up his hand for silence, but it was no use. The students slapped their thighs and hooted.

"If I had my own toilet, I would take care of it, too," called out Izzy, always quick with a joke. This brought a fresh burst of laughter.

The tiny, three-room apartment that held Sol's five-person family did not have a bathroom. Down the hall, two toilets served the four crowded apartments on their floor.

Teacher Weiss was trying not to laugh. He wrote the sentence on the blackboard. "In this sentence," he explained, "'toilet' means washing, dressing, and combing your hair. It's an old-fashioned meaning for that word, but you might still hear it today."

These heavy-handed lessons on the importance of washing and dressing correctly came every couple of weeks. Everyone knew they were sent from the Educational Alliance's investors, uptown German Jews who were already second-generation Americans and felt embarrassed and dishonored by their downtown "cousins," with their old-country ways. Teacher Weiss would be in trouble if he didn't teach these lessons.

"All right, let's finish," Teacher Weiss said. "Number three. In America, people bathe every day, especially in summer."

To bathe, Sol had to go to a public bathhouse and pay for a five-minute shower. Of course, there were separate days for men and women, so bathing every day was impossible.

"*Oy!* It's a shame nobody told our landlord he should provide a bathtub so we can be American," Izzy wisecracked.

"I'll bet he charges you American rent, though," another student said in Yiddish. This earned more sarcastic laughter.

Teacher Weiss gave up. "That will be all for tonight, class," he said. "Pass your slates to the end of the row. I'll see you on Thursday."

Sol was still laughing to himself as he left the classroom.

"Mr. Lefkowitz?" a female voice asked. Sol turned. Emotion immediately flooded his body.

It was Rose, from the tourist boat. Her lightly rouged lips smiled and her hazel eyes were friendly under their arched brows. She wore a thin blouse with short, lacy sleeves. It showed off her body much better than the mannish shirt she'd worn on the cruise.

In the two weeks since then, Sol had thought of Rose often. All during the time he'd talked with her father, he'd been aware of her, felt her eyes on him. He was sure that just as his sister Hanna had suggested, Rose had thought he was handsome.

And she, he noticed now, while not really beautiful, had a glow of well-being that made her seem so. How clean and cool her skin looked! He hadn't visited the bathhouse in two days. The rich people who supported the school—her people—thought his people were unwashed and smelled bad. He flushed as this thought crossed his mind, making him sweat.

The hall had already been filled with people when Sol's English class ended. Rose said something, but her voice was drowned out by the noise of feet and voices.

"Sorry, I didn't hear...." Sol turned his ear towards her.

"It's certainly busy in here," Rose said directly into his ear. "Would you like to walk outside?"

She smelled of some flowery soap and her warm breath tickled. He'd never been this close to a woman outside of his family.

"Yes, sure," he said, his voice uneven.

She smiled and turned towards the stairs to the street. Sol followed.

On the way to the stairs, they passed a classroom where men were setting out their tools to begin a class on furniture upholstering. In another classroom women and a few men were taking their places at rows of electric sewing machines for a training class in garment-factory work.

Descending the three flights of stairs, they passed through areas of competing sounds: barked commands and stamping feet from the gymnasium, a choral group in the theater, and violins and brass instruments in small practice rooms. On the first floor, there was a buzz of talk and quick laughter from the young men's and young women's parlors. A more intense rumble of voices came from the room where the old men studied the same ancient Hebrew texts that Sol had studied in high school. They never tired of arguing about what the ancient rabbis had really meant.

In the suddenly empty first-floor hallway, the temperature inside the grand stone building was almost comfortable. But outside on the street, the pavement radiated back all the heat it had absorbed from the July sun. The light was fading from the sky, although the lamp lighter had not yet lit the gas streetlights.

When Sol walked with his stepmother or Hanna, he had to remember to shorten his steps, but Rose walked more swiftly, at a speed equal to his. They turned south through the shadowy streets, towards the restaurants and bars where young people hung out in the evenings. Why had she come? Sol wondered. Although he'd thought of her, daydreamed of meeting her somewhere, he'd certainly not expected her to show up at his English class.

As if she heard his thoughts, Rose spoke.

"When we met on the boat, my father asked you about your English class. I was wondering what it was like."

"Oh!" Had she been listening at the door? For how long?

"I was only there for about ten minutes," she said, again answering his thought. "I heard you reading aloud from *Paul Revere's Ride*. You read well."

"Thank you." Sol felt his cheeks color again and he was glad of the semidarkness. He had practiced the Longfellow poem at home, enjoying its marching rhythm, reciting it for his two younger brothers until they walked away in boredom.

"You're not working on the boat anymore?" Rose asked. "The Irish fellow told me."

She had gone to the pier, then, looking for him? He wondered what Jimmy had said about him. "I'm not a very good salesman," he admitted.

"I suppose you have to be really pushy to do that sort of job," she said. "You don't seem like that kind of person. You seem more…thoughtful."

Sol tried not to feel flattered. "There are not many jobs for thoughtful immigrants with not-so-good English, Miss Koestlic," he said.

"Please…Rose."

"And I am Sol," he said.

"So, you are out of work?" she asked.

"There are always jobs in home factories while I look for something better." He was, in fact, stitching shirt cuffs on a treadle sewing machine in the workshop where his stepmother worked. She had given him the place she'd finally earned at a machine and moved back down to basting so they could both work. Men never basted. He wasn't nearly as fast as she was on the machine, though, so she took over during the lunch break to help him make his quota.

"You'll have your own business someday," Rose said warmly. "I can see it."

Sol smiled and shook his head. He could not imagine a way that that would happen. At the moment, he was struggling to get fast enough at sewing shirt cuffs so that he would have a little time left in the day to look for a better job.

"Can you see what kind of business it will be?" he asked, still smiling.

"Something out of the ordinary," Rose said. "Something clever."

Her vision touched him. She hardly knew him, and yet she saw a quality in him that made him special.

"And what about you?" he asked. Then he could have bitten his tongue. Perhaps that question was rude! Surely, she would be expecting to marry, and soon. Probably she would not have an arranged marriage, as was the custom with the Russian Jews. She would likely be courted and would choose her husband. Or, as he secretly hoped would happen to him, she would marry for love. Either way, his question stepped into territory where he was ignorant and likely to blunder.

But Rose did not appear to be the least bit offended.

"Oh, I'm going to university in the fall," she said. "Barnard."

Sol was shocked into silence.

In America, he'd learned, marriage for love was normal. It wasn't even unheard of in Russia. His father and mother's marriage had been for love, rather than arranged. Although, when his father was ready to remarry after Sol's mother died, he had hired a matchmaker. "Romance is for the young, when you're still learning," he'd told Sol years later. "I already knew how to be married. Anyway, at my age I didn't have time for all that."

However, a university education for a woman was completely outside Sol's experience. Certainly, all the young Jewish women in his neighborhood could read. They read prayer books in Yiddish and if they were interested in politics they read the Yiddish newspaper, *The Jewish Daily Forward*. There were women who wished for more education—his own sister, Hanna, for example. But he had never met a woman who read books by Sigmund Freud! It made Rose even more intriguing.

All the same, a pang of jealousy struck his heart. How could she mention such a breathtaking leap—university—in such a casual tone? "That's…wonderful," he said, fumbling for the word. He felt jealous; it was a new and different feeling to be jealous of a woman. "What will you study?"

"*I* want to be an architect!"

The defiance in her tone had been clear. "Is there someone who doesn't want this?"

"Papa has a different idea about what I should study."

"Ah."

She looked at him sharply, perhaps thinking that he agreed with her father. He gave her a twisted smile. They had something in common, after all, he thought. They both had big dreams that were blocked. In her case, her father opposed the future that she had chosen. Sol's case was different. He knew his father was on his side; Avram only wanted his son to achieve the most that he could. Even making Sol spend the year working his way through elementary school, humiliating as it had been, had been a way for him to get a good, nonreligious foundation in English. What blocked Sol was prejudice against Jews and against the specific kind of Jew that he was—Eastern European.

Ahead, at the corner of Delancey Street, people stood in groups on the sidewalk. Sol and Rose turned the corner and entered a throng.

"Hey! Sol!"

It was Izzy, from class. He had turned from a group of their fellow students. His eyes, under raised eyebrows, zigzagged back and forth from Sol to Rose.

"Uh, Izzy, this is Rose," Sol said.

Rose stuck out her hand. Izzy blinked shyly at it. A sweet little smile played on his lips as he shook her hand politely.

"Isadore Aronov," he said formally.

"Rose Koestlic," she replied.

"Oh? Related to Herbert Koestlic?"

"My father."

Izzy's dark eyebrows shot up again and his pale blue eyes widened. "He sent you to watch our class?"

"To spy, you mean? Because he's a donor?" The meaning behind Izzy's questions had gone right over Sol's head, but Rose had caught it immediately. "Not a bit. I came to see Sol. We met when he was working on a tour boat. Actually, Papa doesn't even know I'm here." She grinned.

Both Izzy and Sol digested this last information for three full seconds. Then Izzy burst out laughing. "Very pleased to meet you, Miss Koestlic," he said, with a small bow.

Sol was trying to decide how he felt. If his sister Hanna had gone by herself to another part of town to see a young man—before she was married, that is—or, well, even after she was married, and not told their father…. Of course, Hanna would never have done such a thing. He felt as though icy sparks were dancing on his scalp at the mere thought that Rose had taken such a risk to visit him.

Or was that the reason she'd come? He reminded himself of the disagreement with her father that she'd mentioned. And that Rose did not live by the same rules that he did.

"Rose will go to Barnard in the fall to study architecture!" Sol blurted.

Izzy's smile vanished. "*Zol zayn mit mazl,*" he said: *Good luck.* He raised a finger. "I'm going to change my name from Aronov to Arondorff," he said, replacing the Russian ending with a German one. "Columbia University too admits Jews… *if* they are the better, German type."

"It's very unfair, of course," Rose said at once. "I believe everyone should be allowed to study and become whatever they want to be!"

"I want to be a landlord," Izzy declared. "I want to collect rent every week and tell my tenants that there are *no* rats on my property—I don't allow them!" He brightened, theatrically. "Maybe you'll design a beautiful building for me, and I'll manage it," he said.

Rose laughed. "I'd like that."

Izzy nodded his head towards the circle of classmates behind him. Most of them were listening to an older man who was passionately expressing an opinion in Yiddish.

"Would you like to be introduced?" he asked Rose. Sol's spirits sank. Izzy's chatter was light and amusing. But once the socialists, the unionists, and the general doomsayers got Rose's attention, Sol wouldn't get another second of time with her. And she'd probably never come back.

But Rose leaned her head towards Sol. "Were you thinking of having a coffee?" she murmured.

"Yes, certainly. Let's go in." he said quickly, his mood bouncing upward again.

"Maybe next time," Rose told Izzy.

Inside, it smelled of coffee, apples, and cinnamon. An apple strudel must have just come out of the wide, black oven that radiated heat from the far corner of the large room. Rose walked part way towards the back, then repelled by the heat, turned and chose a table near the door.

Sol, meanwhile, had been thinking fast.

"Uh...I meant to ask Izzy something," he said. "Please, stay right here. I'll be back in a second."

He rushed back outside.

"Izzy, please, can you lend me a quarter?" he said rapidly in Yiddish.

"A quarter? What makes you think I have that much? I'm not a landlord yet!"

"Twenty cents? What do you have?"

"My friend," Izzy began. He put his hand on Sol's shoulder. "This is an excellent moment to ask yourself an important question. Can you afford that woman?"

"I only want to buy her a cup of coffee," sputtered Sol. "She just showed up, I wasn't expecting her. Oh, come on, Izzy! I'll pay you back tomorrow."

"I really don't have any money," Izzy said regretfully, "or I'd be in there having a piece of that strudel I smell."

Sol sighed deeply.

"Well, well, let's see," Izzy said, patting Sol's shoulder. "Fellows!" he called out, turning to the group. He didn't need to call for their attention, though; by now, all eyes were on Sol and Izzy. "Who's got a few pennies to lend this poor man? Name your terms! He's desperate."

There was laughter, some scolding tch-tch's, and one disapproving whistle, all proof that although no one had appeared to notice Sol and Rose before, everyone had. Hands went into pockets. Coins passed around the circle towards Izzy, who slowly counted them out into Sol's cupped palms. "Fifteen, sixteen…a nickel? You have a wealthy donor!" he exclaimed. "Twenty-two, twenty-four…come on, boys, who's got one more penny to make it twenty-five?"

"No, no, this is fine," Sol muttered. But a short, red-headed young man dug another coin out of his pants pocket and passed it around. "Thank you, thank you!" Sol said. "I'll pay everyone back in class on Thursday!" He gave the group one of his best smiles and hurried back into the coffee house. He'd been gone much longer than he'd intended.

Florence, Rivka's daughter, was just setting two cups of coffee and two plates, each covered with an enormous slice of strudel, on the table in front of Rose. Florence gave Sol a side-look as she left.

Speechless, Sol clutched the coins in his fist.

"Hello," Rose said. "Dutch treat," she added, sweeping her hand over the food. She took in his half-open mouth, his silence. "Oh dear…I hope it's all right? Oh, I shouldn't have done this, should I? I'm sorry!"

"No….No, it's fine," Sol said, in English. "I can take care of it. But what is, '*Dutch treat*'?"

Rose blinked. "It means we each pay for our own instead of one of us paying for all of it. That's just how my friends and I do it. But I shouldn't have assumed that you wanted strudel. I see that."

In fact, Sol had never eaten a whole piece of Rivka's strudel all by himself. Even back when he was working on the docks and had a little pocket money, he and two friends would always divide a seven-cent piece into three pieces, flipping a coin to see who had to pay the extra penny. He'd borrowed enough from Izzy to cover one piece for the two of them to split.

To compose himself, Sol went and poured two glasses of water from the pitcher on the counter. He hadn't intended to order coffee, either. He had to get up for work at six, with the rest of the family. A cup of weak tea would have been fine, and would have only cost two cents, instead of five.

"Are all of your friends going to university?" he asked, when he sat down again. He picked up his fork and took a bite of the strudel.

"Oh, no," Rose said. "Well, some of the young men. Not the girls."

"So you are unusual?"

A teasing smile quirked the corners of her lips. "Very!" she said.

She was flirting with him. Sol knew he should say something light and a little bit daring, something Izzy would say. But instead, he spoke his true feeling.

"I admit that. I, too, sometimes feel I want a different life than my friends do— a more educated life."

She smiled and looked pleased.

"You are also very nice," he added quickly.

"Thank you. My friends are nice, too, but I'm afraid they don't want to do anything interesting with their lives. They don't want to have any fun now, either," she added, then drew in her breath as if to stop herself from saying any more. She shot a quick, sideways look at Sol, then pushed a forkful of strudel into her mouth.

Sol wondered what she meant by 'fun.' One moment she seemed mature and confident and the next moment she was like a twelve-year-old, plugging food into her mouth to stop her words. It was charming. They sipped their drinks and poked at their strudel. His eyes kept returning to the soft curls that had escaped her loose top knot.

"I don't think I can finish this," Rose said. "I didn't know it would be so filling. It's not like German strudel at all."

"I'm full, too," Sol said. He was amazed to see that he'd drunk more than half of his coffee. Because of that, he would toss in his blanket on the sofa, unable to sleep, until three a.m. Sighing, he went to find Florence and bought oiled squares of cloth to wrap the leftovers.

"I saw that coming," Florence said.

The squares of cloth were five for a penny. He had already spent thirteen cents!

Rose stared at the cloth, puzzled, when he put it next to her plate.

"Take the rest home?" she said when he explained. "Oh…would you like mine, too? Do you have little brothers or sisters? Take mine for them, please!"

He realized she had intended to just leave the rest. What would it be like, he wondered, to feel that you didn't have to eat everything on your plate? That you could throw food away.

Rose pulled at a chain attached to a loop on her skirt. A small, delicately enameled watch came out of her pocket. It startled Sol—her own timepiece, so tiny and so beautiful!

"Oh, my goodness!" she cried. "It's almost eight-thirty. If I'm not home by nine, Papa will start telephoning my friends!"

"We'd better get going," he said. He didn't know how far away she lived, but he doubted they could get there in half an hour. They could run to the Grand Street Station of the new Second Avenue subway line, but who knew how long it would take for a train to arrive? And anyway, he no longer had the money for the fare. When he borrowed twenty-five cents, that included one five-cent fare north for each of them and a return five-cent fare south for him. As soon as he'd heard that Rose had come downtown by herself, he'd resolved to accompany her home and make sure she got there safely. But that money had been spent on strudel. What would he do now?

Rose was already making for the door.

Sol chased her. "Here!" he said, "for my food." He handed her twelve cents, although it hardly seemed fair, as she'd given him half of hers.

"What? Oh!—all right. Which street has the most traffic?"

"Huh? Come this way! The Grand Street Station is only three blocks." He was searching through his pockets, hoping to find a nickel. Maybe she'd go Dutch on the fare?

"Station?" She was looking wildly around, up and down the street. "There's one. What luck!" She darted into the street, flinging one arm into the air. "Taxi!"

By the time Sol had regained his wits, the motorcar was pulling over.

"Wait! What are you doing? I certainly can't pay for a taxi…"

But Rose already had the door open. She turned to face him. "Sol," she said. "It was so nice to be with you. Would you like to meet again?"

"Yes, I would," Sol said in surprise, and surprised himself further by adding, "very much."

"Good." Rose's smile was pleased. "I would, too." She reached up and almost, but not quite, touched his face. Then she climbed into the cab and pulled the door shut.

Sol stood watching the yellow-paneled rear of the taxi as it wove around horse-pulled carriages. She had destroyed every idea he'd formed about how this unexpected meeting should go. And he was already thinking of things he wanted to say to her the next time they met.

Chapter 6
2009

Seth was already half an hour late.

"It figures," Miri said. "This time, he didn't call me asking to meet. I called him."

"He's difficult," Dalia agreed. "Defensive." They were waiting in the sitting area of Miri's tiny studio apartment.

"But I told him I could definitely help him." Miri had to raise her voice over the grumble of the ancient air conditioner. It was a hot Saturday afternoon.

Dalia petted the seafoam-green cotton blanket that Miri had used to cover a horrible orange chair. "I love the color you used here," she said. "It's relaxing."

Miri made a face. She was lying on her fake leather sofa. She hated the feel of it. She hated the view of a brick wall out the apartment's only window. But small and crummy as this apartment was, she still couldn't afford it on the tiny salary she made at the gallery. She wanted to grow up, be an adult, support herself, but she couldn't, not yet. She had to take money from her father, who reminded her every month that he'd told her: studying art was a bad choice.

"If you were about to say that I should have been an interior decorator—don't," she said. "That's one of my dad's lines."

Dalia picked up the can of mixed nuts they'd been passing back and forth and raised her eyebrows. It was empty. Miri tilted her chin defiantly. Her lips still tingled from the salt. Usually, Dalia would have been the one who finished the nuts. But today Miri was feeding her stress.

She and Dalia had only really gotten to know each other when Miri moved to New York to go to graduate school. They were seven years apart, an age difference that had been as wide as an ocean when they were girls.

Dalia had grown up just north of New York City, just outside the town of Battle Hill. Their great-grandfather's business still operated there, although the family didn't own it anymore. Their great-aunt Rina, the youngest of their great-grandfather's children, had run it with her husband until she was in her late 70's.

Dalia had been the kind of child who demanded to be the center of attention. She had gloried in the attention with which her indulgent aunts and uncles rewarded her—Aunt Rina, in particular. Miri, on the other hand, had been as shy as Dalia was bold. Her family had moved to St. Louis before she was old enough to walk, but her mother brought her to Battle Hill once or twice a year for Passover seders and other family occasions. As the youngest child, she had had to ask The Four Questions at the seder. The relatives had fussed over her without mercy, tormenting her with praise in the belief that it would make her more self-confident. She remembered both envying and resenting her fearless cousin.

If she hadn't been so lonely when she started graduate school in New York, she never would have returned Dalia's phone message. But it turned out that the grown-up lawyer-Dalia was not like the teen-aged Dalia. She'd become a good listener. She sympathized and gave out hope. Miri's mother was focused on her own mid-life problems and wasn't available for sympathy. But at least Miri had Dalia.

The sharp *brrring!* of the bell from the building's lobby made Miri jump. She rolled her eyes. It was about time!

"Yes?" she said into the intercom.

"Seth."

She buzzed him in. In a moment, the clank of the elevator on its way down to the street level came through the wall.

"Remember," Dalia said, "our first priority is to find out where he got the drawing. And let's hope he's calmer than last time."

Miri sighed. The truth was, she was a little afraid of Seth. That's why she'd asked Dalia to be there.

She watched through the peep-hole in her door as he stepped out of the elevator with the brown paper shopping bag under his arm. He looked sweaty and tired. Maybe after the subway ride and the walk to her apartment in the ninety-five-degree heat, he wouldn't have the energy to be angry.

"Hi," she said, opening the door. "Glass of ice-water?"

"Thanks." He took a couple of steps towards the couch before he noticed Dalia and stopped short.

"Hi," Dalia said, mildly. "I'm your cousin, Dalia Blostok. I called you when you moved back to Battle Hill."

"You're the lawyer."

Miri had opened the refrigerator and was pulling a plastic ice cube tray from the tiny freezer compartment. She couldn't see Dalia's expression, but she fully expected a cutting remark.

To her surprise, Dalia only sighed.

"Yes, a lawyer."

Once in a while, for no obvious reason, Dalia sank into a glum tone, especially about her job.

"She invited you to be here?" Seth asked.

"Yup. Apparently, you got angry last time."

Seth puffed out his breath. "I'm not angry now. And, um, I think this is a private matter."

"Well, it can't stay private, or you'll never sell that drawing."

Miri shut her eyes. Now, surely, Seth would explode.

When she turned from the refrigerator, his face was working: he was struggling with Dalia's casual admission that she knew about the drawing. Miri imagined how her ex-boyfriend Chuck would have reacted—had reacted, once. He would have picked up the vase on the end table and smashed it on the floor. But Seth only raised his free hand in a gesture of defeat and collapsed onto the sofa. The brown shopping bag flopped down next to him.

In fact, it was Miri who burst out irritably.

"Be careful!" she said. "I can't believe you're treating it that way!"

"Huh?"

She pointed at the bag.

"Carrying that beautiful, delicate drawing around in a shopping bag. It's ridiculous!" There was more authority in her voice than she'd intended.

"How am I supposed to carry it?" Seth asked.

"A briefcase? A suitcase? Tied between two pieces of plywood? It's valuable!"

"Oh," Seth looked sheepish. "I guess you're right. It might be worth real money."

Miri inhaled deeply to calm herself. "It's real art," she said. "It looked like it was in almost perfect condition. You've got to keep it that way."

"Right. You're right," he muttered.

"It's a good disguise, though," Dalia's eyes crinkled with amusement. "No thief would mug you for that bag."

Seth's ears reddened and a blush came out in front of his long sideburns as Miri handed him the glass of ice water. How easy it was to embarrass him! She recalled how his leg had jiggled with nervousness the last time they'd met. Maybe he wasn't as tough as he sounded.

Dalia raised an eyebrow at Miri. *Move on,* her expression said.

"So...," Miri began, "you want to sell the drawing, right? I mean, you don't want to keep it?"

Seth glanced down at the paper bag. An odd look crossed his face. Was it surprise? Regret? Then he twitched his mouth to one side. "What would I do with it?"

Miri turned a chair from the small table and sat down. "Well, before it can be sold, the first thing is that it has to be proved authentic. An expert in American drawings of this time period will look at everything—the overall style, the shape of the curves, the thickness of the lines, the brand of charcoal or ink, the type of paper, the artist's signature..."

"There isn't a signature," Seth said.

"Yes, and that's good! O'Keeffe never signed her work."

Seth squinted at her. "They're looking to see if it's a forgery?"

"Exactly. They also want to know who owned it, the location where it turned up, and if that fits with what is known of the artist's life."

He sucked his top lip into his mouth to stop a question, then opened his mouth to ask it anyway. But Miri wasn't finished.

"AND, it has to be appraised. By a certified appraiser. There was a scandal recently about some supposed O'Keeffe works called The Canyon Suite...."

Seth made an exasperated noise. "There's got to be an easier way than doing all that."

"Why? What's the problem?" Miri asked.

"Don't deal well with The System," he muttered. "Not interested in following The Establishment's rules."

Miri clearly heard capital letters on The System and The Establishment.

"There's the black market," Dalia said helpfully.

Miri rolled her eyes. But Seth looked interested.

"How would that work?"

"If it's money you want, you won't get it by selling on the black market," Miri said quickly. "For a piece like this, by such a famous artist, you'd get ten percent of what you'd get if you sold it legally. Ten percent at the most."

Dalia nodded. "Sounds about right. But ten percent of half a million dollars is still fifty thousand. That's nothing to sneeze at."

"Dalia!" Miri scolded.

Whose side was Dalia on? What kind of game was she playing? Was she baiting Seth, the way lawyers did in court, to make him confess his real motivation for a crime? Obviously, what drove Seth was money — the drawing was just worth cash to him.

A stray thought flew through her mind. *Of course, she'd love more money, too. Especially money that suddenly appeared out of nowhere, like in a dream.*

"Miri?" Dalia said. "Hello?"

"What? Sorry…I wasn't listening."

Dalia shot her an appraising look. "How would he sell it on the black market? Would he take it to a fence? I'm just curious, because I could get some names…."

"How would I know?" Miri snapped. "I'm not up on black market sales. I guess he'd find some big drug dealer. They buy black market art."

Seth looked surprised. "Drug dealer? Seriously?"

A bit sourly, she explained. "They collect stolen art. If they're arrested, they offer to give the art back in return for a lower-level charge. It works because in return for the lower charge, the police can take credit for finding the art. Plus, buying stolen art is an easy way to get rid of extra drug profits."

Sell the O'Keeffe drawing to a drug dealer? Why was she even talking about that?

"Well, this isn't stolen," Seth said.

"No?" Dalia cut in coolly. "Then how'd you get it?"

Seth crossed his arms in front of his chest and scowled.

"Let me guess," Dalia said. "You found it in a trash can."

"Almost," Seth said, then pressed his lips together.

"In a thrift shop? Garage sale? Oh, I know…." Dalia pasted a grin on her lips. "The artist was selling it in a street market and you put it in an old frame thinking you'd fool everyone."

Seth sighed. "No, it really is old. It has to be." His face worked. "OK, I'll tell you. I found it in this little old house we're tearing down. It was in the attic behind a layer of insulation and some boards covering the rafters."

"In Battle Hill?" Dalia said.

"Yeah."

"Is this down in the flat part of town? What's the address?"

"Thirty-two Marsh Street. Why?"

Dalia's expression seemed to freeze, and she missed a beat of the conversation. The extra half-second of silence allowed Miri to put in a question.

"No sales receipt, or anything?" she asked.

Seth just gave her a side-eye.

Dalia raised her elbow slightly in Miri's direction and Miri got the message: *Quiet.*

She took a deep breath. Her heart was starting to pound. From what Seth had just said, the drawing had to be old. It looked like the right age for an early O'Keeffe. Only, there were no documents and the ownership was unclear. So even if the experts thought it was an O'Keeffe, it might be impossible to prove it. And there had to be proof, solid proof, for it to be accepted by the legitimate art world. Without proof, the boost to her career and more importantly, the very existence of a new piece of work by Georgia O'Keeffe, would all fade away to nothing.

Dalia was chewing her knuckle. "Marsh Street? So who owns this house?" she asked.

"My boss. Maybe."

"*'Maybe?'*"

Seth sighed. "This is why I'm not working today," he said. "The deal is, my boss got a tip that that whole area is going to be rezoned for industrial use. He bought the house and everything in it—well, almost everything—from an old lady. His cousin works at a bank and will give him an extra-big mortgage loan on that property. He'll use that to buy a couple of more houses on the street. The cousin will fix him up with mortgages on those. He and his cousin will buy up as many as they can. If they get control of a whole area, they can sell it to a big company that wants to build on it. For a ton of money. Only thing is, he has to tear down the houses each time before he can get the next loan. That's what the bank requires."

"And?" Dalia asked. "Why aren't you working today? What's stopping him from this sweet little deal with his cousin the banker?"

"The old lady," Seth said. "She claims he sold some piece of furniture before she could get it out of there. She says it was a family heirloom, and the contract said she had the right to it. She's suing him and threatening to cancel the sale."

"Family heirloom?" Dalia murmured. "On Marsh Street? So, you're saying that the house may or may not belong to your boss. And that the old woman may or may not know that this piece of art was up in the attic."

Seth pulled at one of his sideburns. "She hasn't mentioned any art. She's just bent out of shape about an old sewing machine."

"Oh, my," Dalia murmured. "And does your boss know you took the drawing?"

Miri breathed a tiny sigh of relief. She'd gotten lost in the story Dalia was drawing out of Seth. But finally, Dalia was bringing her questions around to what she and Miri had agreed was crucial — had Seth stolen the drawing?

"Sure," Seth said, to Miri's surprise. "I showed it to him."

"Oh? And you asked him if you could have it?"

"Yeah. He said fine. He thought it was really ugly."

Miri was indignant. Dalia laughed.

"So he's not a sophisticated art lover," she said. "Did you get his signature on that?"

"Huh? No. He just said sure, take it. *I* kind of like it," he added, defensively.

Miri let out a groaning breath. "You'll have to get him to sign something."

"Actually…," Dalia was looking at her nails. "As I was saying before, a quick sale on the black market would be easiest."

"*What?*" The idea of fast, easy money had loosened Miri's moral sense when Dalia first brought up selling the drawing on the black market. But now, suddenly, her morals snapped back firmly in place.

"What are you talking about, Dalia? That's dirty money. And this gorgeous piece of art that I'm sure is a Georgia O'Keeffe would disappear into a bank vault! No one would ever know about it!"

Dalia shrugged. "Money is money, and I think that's what Seth wants. To be perfectly honest, I need money myself. And you, Miri—you're always moaning about your student loan and your pitiful salary. Admit it—you'd welcome a little money, too."

"Whoa! Now wait just a minute." Seth's eyes had darkened. He roughly jerked the paper bag onto his lap.

Miri winced.

"If that's the way you're going to be, I'm leaving." He stood.

"If that's the way *you're* going to be, you're not going to get very far," Dalia said.

"Huh? Why? What are you going to do, call the police?"

Dalia clicked her tongue. "No. If you want to leave, go ahead. But the fact is, you need our help. Number one, even a drug lord isn't going to buy a drawing that could be a fake. It has to be certified by an expert, and Miri can get that for you without raising any suspicion. And number two, how are you going to find this drug lord to sell it to? I actually know lawyers who defend those creeps—Rocky Silverman comes to mind, for one. I can get you a good connection. And I think that's worth something to you."

Seth poked his jaw forward and opened his mouth to speak. Then he closed his mouth and locked eyes with Dalia. They stared hard at each other for a long moment.

"What do you want?" he finally said.

"Twenty percent for each of us," Dalia said promptly.

"Fifteen."

Dalia shrugged. "Done. Miri, can I have a piece of paper and a pen? I want a signed agreement on that."

Miri took a deep breath, pushing down the horror that had been growing in her chest. *What had she been thinking of before?* What really mattered to her was discovering a new O'Keeffe. It was what she'd trained for, what she'd defied her father to be able to do. *Do what you've chosen to do*, she told herself. *Live the life you want.*

"Absolutely not." Her voice came out shakily at first, then rose and grew stronger until she was practically shouting. "Are you out of your mind? I don't want anything to do with this. Not *anything*! You need to leave, Dalia. You need to go. *Now!*"

Chapter 7
1909

The week after he had coffee with Rose, Sol walked twenty blocks north to the ladies garment factories along Twenty-third Street. It had taken him five days to find out where Mr. Koestlic's factory was located and to build up the courage to go there.

Koestlic's office was on the ninth floor of the building. The factory workrooms were on the four floors below that. There was a small, private elevator to the ninth floor, but it required a key to operate, so Sol climbed nine flights of stairs.

The stairwells on the factory floors were open to the workrooms. On the fifth floor, men stood around long tables guiding electric cutters through thick stacks of fabric. A haze of lint filled the air. If a fire started on this floor, it would roar up the stairwell quickly, trapping everyone above. The sixth and seventh floors were noisy. Rows of women and a few men bent over hundreds of black Singer sewing machines. The machines hummed and clacked; people shouted to each other. On the eighth floor, women of all ages sat sewing buttonholes or stood at ironing boards pressing finished items with electric irons.

The ninth floor, however, was different. Unlike the landings of the four lower floors of Koeslic's business, this landing was enclosed. From the moment he passed through the door, a motionless, straight-backed woman pinned him with her gaze. Her hands were suspended over the keys of a tall, black typewriter. When he got close enough, she spoke.

"We're not hiring," she announced angrily.

Sol's stomach knotted in terror. At the same time, one of Mendel's lessons on dealing with people popped into his mind: *Be confident; it puts people at ease.*

"It's all right," Sol said, forcing his voice to sound calm. "Mr. Koestlic knows me. His daughter Rose does, too. I just need to have a word with him. Please tell him Sol Lefkowitz is here."

The woman bent forward abruptly. Sol imagined he could hear her corset creak. "*You* know *Rose*?" She looked him up and down. With her mouth pressed into a straight line, she stood and disappeared through a doorway. In half a minute, she reappeared and waved him in.

The dark red carpet was so thick that Sol almost tripped when he stepped through the door. Mr. Koestlic sat behind a large wooden desk. His eyebrows were drawn together in a frown but relaxed when he saw Sol's face.

"You!" he said. "The young fellow so interested in Sigmund Freud. What do you mean by using my daughter's name to get in to see me? You gave me a scare! I thought she'd been kidnapped."

"Kid-napped?"

"Stolen. Taken. Held for money," Mr. Koestlic said.

"By *me*?"

"Well? What's your business, then?"

"Uh…" *Show people you like them,* Mendel had taught him. *Offer to help them.* Sol swallowed. "I enjoyed talking with you," he said. "I thought I would like to be part of your company. I'm a good worker."

Mr. Koestlic raised an eyebrow. "You want a job," he said.

"Yes."

"Mr. Lefkowitz," Mr. Koestlic said slowly. "You are a clever young man."

"Thank you."

"You read books. You're interested in theories. Yes?"

"Yes, of course. Everyone is."

"No, everyone isn't. Let me tell you two things, Mr. Lefkowitz. First, I don't have any job openings right now. And second, this is not a union shop, and I don't want it to become one. I don't need ideas, I need hands. Fast hands that don't think."

"But I'm not in the union."

Mr. Koestlic stood. "Good day, Mr. Lefkowitz," he said. He tapped a silver counter bell that sat on his desk: *DING!*

"No, you don't under…"

"Good day," Mr. Koestlic repeated.

The door to the office opened.

"This way," the terrifying woman said.

Sol stumbled out, confused. How had that gone wrong? Why had Mendel's advice failed? For the first time, it occurred to him that Mr. Koestlic might tell Rose he had come. Would she think he had used her to get a job? That hadn't been what he'd meant to do.

ooo

By the time he reached home, he felt completely wrung out.

"Sol, come sit down," his stepmother, Matya, said. "I need to talk with you."

Matya sat at the kitchen table mending the elbow of Avram's clean work shirt. A high-necked, floor-length dress encased her stout figure, and a *tichel* covered her hair completely. Only her stubby blond eyelashes behind her glasses reminded him that her hair was blond. The glasses gave her a refined and educated look, while the gap between her front teeth when she smiled suggested worldly experience. But Sol knew that both of those signals were false. Actually, she was not interested in knowledge or non-spiritual things. She was a narrowly religious woman, although she did not apply the rules of Orthodox Judaism unkindly.

"Sit," she said again. "I have something to tell you."

Sol sighed.

"I asked for work at four places today," he said tiredly.

"Good! I can see that you are really trying. I'm sure a job will come along soon."

Sol blinked and sat down. Matya continued stitching calmly, her head bent down so he couldn't see her eyes. But he sensed tension in her body.

"What is it, then?"

Matya cleared her throat. "Sol, you're nineteen, a handsome young man. I'm sure there are young women who have their eyes on you. Today I had a meeting with the *shadkhanit*."

Sol drew back in his chair. "Shimmel the Shirtman?"

Shimmel was the matchmaker. He seemed to own a hundred shirts, each more beautiful than the last. It was rumored that a custom-made shirt could insure a young woman a match with the man she fancied, but no one had ever admitted to bribing him.

"You want me to get married? I can't support a wife."

"The marriage won't happen immediately," she said. "But it will be good for you to be engaged."

Sol felt sweat trickling down his sides, and it was not from the August heat.

"I'm not ready to get married," he said, "and if I were, I would not have the *shadkhanit*. My parents didn't have an arranged marriage, and neither will I. I will choose my own wife."

Matya looked up at him. Her mouth was set determinedly.

"Your father and I want you to have a sanctified marriage to a woman who knows how to keep a proper Jewish household. Someone who will bring up your children with the religious training that you've had. You have no idea how to find such a woman."

Anger flashed through Sol. *"Your father and I,"* – *phooey!* Marrying him off, just as she'd done with Hanna, was clearly Matya's wish. He wanted to pound his fist on the kitchen table. He wanted to laugh in Matya's face. But most of all, in a shining moment, he knew exactly whom he wanted to marry: Rose.

ooo

That Thursday, Sol was the first one out of the classroom door. As he looked up and down the hall, his heart, which had been beating hard with expectation, went still. His chest felt as empty as a field of mown wheat in winter. Rose was not waiting for him as she had been the week before.

"Coming to the meeting at Rivka's tonight?" Izzy called out as he passed Sol.

"No." Sol's voice sounded hollow, even to him.

Izzy turned back. He put his hand on Sol's shoulder. "Oh, come on. I'm telling you, Sol, if you joined the union they'd fix you up with a job in no time."

Sol heard this at home, often. He still didn't understand how his father, who had been a shop keeper—an employer!—had become such a fervent supporter of unions.

"I don't have any money to pay the dues," he told Izzy. "I need the job first."

Izzy snorted and shook his head. "Well then, come to Rivka's and ask around. Save yourself some shoe leather. Someone there will give you a tip."

"Oh, all right," Sol muttered.

He had hoped so much that Rose would be standing outside the classroom today. Hadn't she asked if he wanted to meet again? Hadn't he said yes? If she didn't come to him, he didn't know how to get hold of her.

Izzy squeezed his arm. "Come along, my dear *nebbish*," he said. "I'm inviting you into the meeting. How about some enthusiasm? Not to mention a thank you."

"Sorry," Sol said. "It's good of you. Thanks." But Izzy was already weaving through the crowded hallway, calling out to this person and that person. Sol followed with dragging feet. As the mass of students swept him down the stairs, he thought he would just slip away and go home. He wasn't in the mood to chat with people about a job.

But when he reached the door to the street, Izzy was waiting for him. He linked arms with Sol and set off energetically. Sol was forced to walk faster than usual. After one block, Izzy released his arm but kept up the brisk pace.

The exercise made Sol's heavy mood begin to lift. A cool evening breeze brushed his cheek.

Lately, Avram, who worked in a unionized factory, had talked more and more at dinner about unfair conditions at work. This resulted in silent, tense meals. Matya did not have much patience with talk of strikes and group negotiations. She had only worked in tiny, home workshops, set up in the kitchen or parlor of someone's apartment. Those workshops weren't unionized. For relief of her problems, she relied on prayer.

As Sol's only experience with the garment industry was his family, he assumed most women felt as his stepmother did. However, as he and Izzy neared Essex Street, he was surprised by the buzz of female voices that reached him from over a block away. As they drew closer, one voice stood out from the others.

"…six months, nine months, they keep us 'learning,' at half the pay we should be getting," a young woman raged to a group of women and men. "They dock our pay for the electricity to run their machines! We have to rent the very chairs we sit on! Those bastards are sucking the life out of us!"

Her passion stopped Sol in his tracks. 'Learning?' Why did she say that word with such scorn? Izzy grabbed his arm again and pulled him through the throng.

Inside the coffee house, every seat was taken. Izzy pushed around the edges of the room and found a spot for the two of them to stand near the speakers' table. The officials of the local union, gathered behind the table, were arguing in low voices.

"If the women want to strike, let them," Sol heard. "It will be a good test. We can watch and see how it goes."

"What about 'All for one and one for all?'" another man asked

The first man sighed impatiently.

Someone touched Sol's arm. Rivka's daughter, Florence, handed him a light blue envelope. His name was beautifully hand-written on it with blue ink. Florence blew him a kiss and rolled her eyes.

Sol's heart leaped. Fumbling, he tore open the envelope and drew out a sheet of matching paper.

Dear Sol,

I hope you don't think it is too forward of me to write to you, but I have been thinking of you. Could you meet me on Saturday afternoon at 59th Street and Fifth Avenue at the entrance to the park? Shall we say 3 o'clock? If you cannot come, I will understand, but I hope to see you.

Rose

Chapter 8

2009

Seth began pushing the drawing back into the Foodtown paper bag.

"Don't *do* that!" Miri ordered. Then she softened her voice. "Let me help you wrap it. I know how."

It wasn't Seth she was angry with; it was Dalia. She hated what Dalia had offered to do, hated the idea of some drug dealer using the gorgeous O'Keefe to bargain his way out of a jail sentence. That was not the purpose of art.

Still, she cared about Dalia very much. As soon as her cousin left, Miri regretted throwing her out. But it was too late.

Pulling a chair over to her closet, she got her box of supplies down from the top shelf. She set the drawing on the end of the breakfast bar countertop and began applying overlapping layers of tape to the glass. This was to prevent damage to the art if the glass were broken.

A minute later, she looked up and was startled to meet Seth's eyes. He'd been watching her, silently.

"Yeah, you do know how," he said, nodding. For the first time, he looked friendly.

"This is one of the jobs of an intern. I've done it a thousand times. Not with anything as wonderful as this piece, though."

Seth lowered his eyes, then looked up again. "There is something special about it, isn't there? I like it, too."

Miri saw an opportunity.

"Then why would you sell it to a drug lord who will just shut it in a safe where no one will see it?"

He shrugged. "Easier. Faster. Fifty thou in my pocket right away."

"So that's all it's about for you? Money?"

Seth hesitated. "I guess so," he said.

"You said it was special."

"Yeah, but I need the money. I had to leave my tools and my wheels behind. I need a high-end Skilsaw and a truck that drives. Then I can get a decent construction job, instead of minimum pay for pulling out old insulation. Anyhow, selling the drawing your way, to a museum or whatever, isn't my way."

"Why not?"

"For one thing, it sounds like it would take months. But mainly, I don't trust your 'experts.'" He put plenty of scorn into his voice. "I'll bust my butt to get them what they want, it will take forever, and they'll probably cheat me anyway. The experts always screw you over. That's my experience. So why not just deal with the criminals?"

"Because it's dirty money and the criminals will cheat you even more."

Seth's jaw poked out stubbornly. "Well, I could use the cash now. Couldn't you? Do you make big bucks at your job? I don't think so."

Miri pressed her lips together. Yes, she'd been tempted when Dalia brought up selling the drawing on the black market. In fact, she still felt pulled in two directions. She wanted to move ahead with her life, to live her dream. The lack of money was just another piece of the struggle, but some days it felt like that was what held her back..

She went back to packing the drawing.

"You said you liked it," she said after a few moments. "What do you like about it? What does it say to you?"

She expected Seth to deny that it had any meaning for him, but instead he ran his fingers through the soft curls of his hair and rubbed the back of his neck.

"I dunno. There's a lot going on in it. Energy rising up? Some of the shapes feel like they're about to bust open. Like something's coming…about to be born, maybe? Something good, I'd say. Nothing dark or bad. Anyway, that's what I feel."

Miri stared at him, amazed. She looked down at the drawing, dimmed by a coating of clear tape, then back up at Seth.

"That's what I feel, too." She continued staring at him. "You are so surprising."

"Why? You think someone who works construction can't understand art?" He was trying to bluster, but suddenly Miri felt that she could see through the tough personality that he put on display. She caught sight of a different, more complicated person inside.

"No, I don't think that about construction workers. What surprised me was that a lot of the time you seem pretty negative, but when you looked at the drawing what you felt was all positive."

Seth looked uncomfortable. "Not a lot of good things have happened to me lately," he muttered.

"I heard about that." Miri slipped protectors onto the corners of the drawing's frame.

"...doubt you know what really happened," he said under his breath as Miri got out the roll of bubble wrap.

"But why would you need that much money?" she went on, stretching the bubble wrap out on the breakfast bar countertop. "Like thirty or fifty thousand dollars, to buy tools and a new truck? You could have yours shipped here for a lot less than that."

There was no answer. Miri glanced up. Seth's face was dark with some emotion. On second glance, she read sadness and...anger?. A flash of fear shot through her belly. Without conscious thought, she moved around the end of the counter so the breakfast bar was between them. At the same moment, she understood the answer to her question.

"You sold your tools and your truck, didn't you? To buy drugs?"

Seth sprang in her direction.

Miri screamed and cringed backward, hitting the refrigerator.

He froze.

"You scare me," she whispered.

"You think I would hurt you?" he asked. He stared at her for a second. The darkness had evaporated from his face, replaced by a mixture of amazement and anxiety. Seth picked up the mostly-wrapped drawing from the counter. "I was going for this."

Not for the first time, Miri regretted the gut reactions that her relationship with Chuck had left her with. *Relax,* she told herself. *Not all men react with hair-trigger violence.*

"I didn't sell my equipment to buy drugs," Seth said. "I sold it to pay for the lawyer my dad got for me. And for the money to move here."

Miri swallowed. "Dalia told me a few things about you.... But I shouldn't have said...."

Seth shook his head. "I came here for a new start. I hoped all that stuff wouldn't follow me. Shows you how stupid I am. People always make judgments based on superficial impressions."

Miri bit her lip. "You deserve a new start. I hope it works out for you."

"Hope is stupid," Seth said. "You just have to deal with whatever The System throws at you."

He stuffed the drawing into the Foodtown bag. "I'll find something better to put it in. I need to protect it—I get that."

He crossed the room and pulled open the apartment door.

"Wait! There's something else I needed to tell you!" she called.

"Another time," Seth said, and pulled the door closed behind him.

Miri dodged around the breakfast bar and ran out the door. But she was too late. The elevator must have been standing open on her floor. Now the door had slid shut and the car was already on its way down.

She'd meant to tell him about the Canyon Suite hoax. It was a good reason why the drawing should be examined by a certified art expert. Well, now that would have to wait until the next time she saw him.

Her apartment felt empty. She threw herself down on the chair covered with the green blanket, the chair that Dalia had admired. Their plan had blown up, along with their year-long connection. The wonderful drawing was still in Seth's possession and thanks to Dalia he wasn't interested in Miri's help anymore. He wanted to dump the drawing on the black market .

Why did Seth call himself stupid, she wondered. She didn't think he was. Why was he so angry? What he called "The System" had caused his life to fall apart. She could understand that much.

But she had the feeling that there was more to it. Underneath his bluster, Seth was a sensitive person. His reaction to the drawing, plus the expression on his face when she'd screamed and hit the refrigerator, told her that. What was The System, anyway?

The trauma from her former boyfriend, Chuck, had left a scar on her. At times it made her react in a way that felt foreign to who she was. What if Seth was the same in some way?

Chapter 9
1909

On Saturday after synagogue, Sol headed north to meet Rose. He paid a nickel to ride the elevated trains to the 59th Street entrance to Central Park. It was the first time he'd ever been past 23rd Street. The Second Avenue El jerked and screeched from stop to stop along tracks high above the sidewalk. He had to change trains twice. It took forever.

At 59th Street, he descended the wooden stairs into an entirely new world. His crowded neighborhood in the Lower East Side contained a variety of old, narrow, brick buildings. Laundry hung across alleys. Vegetables that had fallen off pushcarts lay in the gutters along with horse droppings. Gangs of kids played or fought dodging between vehicles. Where he now stood, on the other hand, was very different. The street was spotlessly clean and at this hour, almost empty. One side was lined with new, grey stone buildings decorated with towers and leaded glass windows. On the other side stood a green wall of trees and beyond that, the mowed lawns and wide paths of Central Park. He heard a bird chirp.

Realizing he was gaping foolishly, Sol shut his mouth and squared his shoulders. He oriented himself, turned right, and set off towards Fifth Avenue.

But what time was it? Rose's note had asked him to meet her at three o'clock. He hurried down the long block searching for a clock, but none of the buildings he passed had a shop window where he might glimpse one.

In Sol's own neighborhood, he would have asked someone for the time, and here was a man coming towards him on the sidewalk. This man wore a three-piece suit and a tie. A bowler hat sat on his head. He tapped a shiny cane on the sidewalk each time he stepped forward on his right foot. The man looked hard at him. Sol realized that his own grey denim jacket was shapeless, his patched shirt was no longer white, and he had no tie. The man passed, leaving Sol feeling worthless.

But then Sol's heart squeezed tight in his chest. Wasn't that slim young woman on the opposite corner Rose? A rigid set to the woman's shoulders made him doubtful. Then the woman pulled something from her skirt pocket and looked down into her hand. The tiny, enameled watch! It *was* Rose. Sol raised his arm and broke into a run.

"Rose!" he called, "Rose!"

She raised one hand.

When he reached her, he saw that she looked different today. There was a darkness in her eyes that he hadn't seen before.

"Am I very late? What's wrong?"

"No...nothing." But her usual calm manner seemed ruffled.

"I'm very sorry, Rose," he offered anxiously. "The train was slow."

She brushed her hand over her face as if to remove a cobweb and took a deep breath. "You didn't do anything to apologize for," she said, taking his arm and smiling up at him, "but consider yourself forgiven." She held his gaze with hers, making him feel a bit light-headed. They entered the park.

Yellow pebbles crunched beneath their feet. Sol was vaguely aware of other people around them, but he hardly noticed them. He was savoring the feeling of Rose holding his arm.

"Have you been here before?" she asked.

He inhaled the smell of plants and tipped back his head to appreciate the green leaves overhead. "No," he said. "It's my first time, but it's almost like a place in my town in Poland."

"Really? There was a park like this? You came from a city, then?"

"No, no. It was a small place. Very small and old-fashioned. Where we Jews lived, the houses were close together around a square. On Thursdays, the market was there. But where the landowner lived, it was like this." He looked around. Now he noticed a dozen people strolling the wide path near them and family groups picnicking on the grass. "Only, no other people. All the trees, the space, only for him."

"And what did you hope for in that life? If you'd stayed there, I mean," Rose asked.

Sol turned back to her in surprise. No one had ever asked him that question. "There was not a lot to hope for in Volnavoda. I hoped to leave. Well, no. I hoped...for more education."

"You wanted to study psychology, I suppose," Rose said.

"Yes." He sighed.

"And you will, some day," she went on. "If that's what you want, I'm sure you will do it."

"How?" He cleared his throat. "I would need a degree from the university."

"Well, yes, you would," Rose said.

"I have no money for that. And they wouldn't let me in, anyway."

"Oh." Rose looked away, her eyebrows raised. "Columbia University, you mean? There's City College. It's almost free and it's a very good school, I believe."

Sol sighed. He didn't think his English was good enough to study at a university. But that wasn't the main problem. "I have two little brothers and my family is feeding me as well. I need to find whatever work I can do."

"Of course," Rose murmured. But she fiddled restlessly with the collar of her shirt. Was it because he'd mentioned his search for work?…Oh!

"I asked your father for a job," he confessed.

She gave him a sharp look. "My father? You want to work for him? Is that why you came? For my help?"

"No! No, I…I just thought…" He bit his lip. He'd thought Mr. Koestlic had told her about the interview. In fact, he didn't even want to talk about getting a job. He wanted to talk about his feelings for her.

But the mention of her father had ignited Rose.

"Good, because I'm sure he wouldn't hire you," she said. Her voice had turned sour. "You're too smart and you have dreams. He's afraid of workers with dreams. They might ask for more money and go on strike."

It took him a moment to grasp that her anger was not at him.

"Anyway, I'm the last person he would listen to about something like that."

"But I wasn't asking you…."

"Father doesn't have much respect for women. He thinks female brains are for making witty dinner conversation, not for meaningful work." Her stride had gotten longer and quicker. She stared ahead, but even from the side he could see the darkness in her eyes that he'd seen when he first arrived.

"So he's afraid of *your* brains, the same as mine?"

She turned to him, surprised, and laughed. "I hadn't thought of it that way."

"Meaningful work," Sol repeated. "You are thinking about a job? For you?"

"Yes, exactly!" She was striding forward again. "You *are* clever, Sol. Father and I had it out at lunch today. He said he won't pay for me to study architecture. Well, we'll see about that!" Sol tried to digest her words while keeping up with her.

"How will you…"

"Rose!" a woman's voice called.

Rose's head snapped to the left and she stopped abruptly. "Charlotte," she said, with no enthusiasm at all.

There was a brief silence.

"How do you do?" the woman, Charlotte, said to Sol, looking him up and down and clearly surprised at what she saw. She was about Rose's age, but dressed more formally in a skirt that brushed the ground, a fussy, ruffled blouse, and gloves. She wore a large straw hat shaped like a cake and decorated with silk flowers. A few yards behind her stood a man in a fashionable suit and shiny leather shoes.

Sol, suddenly unable to speak, bowed slightly, looking sideways at Rose to see what she would do, and thus what he should do.

"Er…Charlotte, this is Mr. Lefkowitz. And this is Miss Brandt," Rose said, quickly. "I'm sorry, Charlotte, we can't stop to chat."

Sol began to reach out to shake hands with Miss Brandt. But Rose tapped sharply on his back to tell him to move on.

Miss Brandt was staring at him.

"Good afternoon," Sol said in what he hoped was proper English.

This caused her mouth to fall open in amazement. Her eyes shifted from him to Rose.

Rose turned and walked away, her quick footsteps crunching on the gravel. Sol followed. Ahead, a dirt path branched off to the right and she swerved onto it. When they had walked fifty yards, he saw that the path led to a park exit; they were approaching Fifth Avenue. He ran a few steps to catch up to her.

"She is a friend of yours?" he asked.

"I've known Charlotte since we were little girls. She's become quite boring," Rose said brusquely.

"One of your boring friends?"

"Yes."

"She thinks I should not be here with you."

"Boring and narrow-minded."

They emerged from the park onto a sidewalk. Obviously still upset, Rose stepped into the street paying no attention to the taxi that was dangerously close. Sol had to grab her arm and pull her back. After the taxi had passed, they crossed the street together.

"For you, it's not a problem if we are together?" he asked.

"Why would it be?"

"We are both Jews, but you are a rich German. I'm a Russian. I have no … no connections. I have no money, no job. Everyone believes they have a big future here, but I don't see anything for me."

"Of course you have a future here," Rose said. "This is America. Everyone has a future. There's nothing special about German Jews except that we've been here two or three generations longer. It's up to you to make your fortune, Sol. There's nothing holding *you* back. If you don't become a psychologist, it will be something else. An idea will come to you—you'll know it when you think of it."

They stood in front of a large furniture store on a strangely deserted sidewalk across from the park. Like a soothing oil, her hopeful words sank deep into his feelings and eased an ache that had started when he'd landed in this country—or even before that. Rose believed he had a special destiny, a future of his own making. Hardly knowing what he was doing, he bent towards her and she lifted her face to him. They kissed.

It was his first kiss, every detail new and unexpected. His world narrowed to the feel of her soft lips, the sensations aroused in him when her lips moved, and the smell of her soap and skin. She pressed closer to him, nibbling at his lips and sighing encouragement.

Intoxicated, Sol reached around her to hold her tighter. Rose stepped back.

"You're so handsome," she breathed. "I wanted to do that since I saw you on the boat that day. And now I have."

She took a calming breath and turned to the tall store window. It held a display of living room furniture. A sign said *The American Colonial Home!*

"That's a pretty room, don't you think?" she said, speaking rapidly. "I love the rug! It gives a hand-crafted touch."

"Mmm," Sol murmured, hardly glancing at the rug.

"Someday you'll live in a house like that, Sol," Rose said.

He managed to kiss her again. *With you?* he almost asked. But something stopped him from actually speaking. Something that wasn't in her eyes? He hardly knew.

"No, that's enough, Sol. You're a lovely man. I wanted to do that, and now I have. Come on, we came here for a walk."

She led him back across the street and into the park where all the people were. For the next hour, she kept up a stream of chatter about the park, about the great city of New York, about her passion for architecture. When they parted at the stairway to the Sixth Avenue elevated train, Sol hadn't succeeded in getting the conversation back to what was really on his mind. *How do you feel about me? Don't you want to hear how I feel about you? Because I want so much to tell you.*

"When will I see you again?" he asked.

"I will send you a note, like I did this time. Goodbye, Sol. It was a lovely afternoon."

He tried to kiss her on the lips, but she kissed him sweetly on the cheek, instead, squeezed his hand, and walked away, leaving him feeling as if he were teetering on the edge of a cliff.

Chapter 10
2009

On Monday, Miri was at work dusting the tops of picture frames when Dalia called. She let the phone buzz seven times before she sighed and tapped the screen. Then her throat locked up and she couldn't say hello.

The silence didn't put Dalia off.

"I want to apologize for what I did on Saturday," Dalia said. "I'm sorry. Can I take you out to lunch?"

Miri took a breath. "I'm too busy," she said stiffly. Then she relented. "Bret is out to lunch. I'm in charge." Bret was having lunch with his friend Marc Rodriguez, whom Miri knew had tried to pass off a forged Goya sketch as real. So far, Bret didn't seem interested in doing anything like that, but he was still friends with Rodriguez.

"Dinner?"

"I don't know where you're coming from, Dalia. I thought I knew you, but now I don't understand."

"Will you give me a chance to explain?"

Miri had suffered alternating waves of anger and depression all weekend after throwing Dalia out of her apartment. Now she felt pulled in a third direction—

forgiveness and a return to the sisterly relationship they'd had before.

"Anyway, the whole situation has changed," Dalia went on. "I have a piece of blockbuster information for you."

Miri snorted. Blockbuster information? Her trust in Dalia was still too shaky for her to be tempted by that.

Still, what could it mean?

"Please, Miri? I want to straighten this out."

Miri let a silence grow while she gave in. At least, she thought, she could extract an expensive meal as revenge. Dalia could afford it. And it didn't necessarily mean she would forgive Dalia. It meant she would listen to what Dalia had to say while eating well.

"I think Dazzled is open on Mondays," she finally said.

Dalia gave a very soft "Hm." She probably understood why Miri had chosen such a trendy, expensive restaurant. But all she said was, "Good. I'll try."

Five minutes later, she texted *only reservation open 5:45*. Since the restaurant was near the gallery, there wasn't enough time for Miri to go home and dress nicely. Her work outfit, artistically mismatched and funky, would have to do.

ooo

Dalia was already waiting inside when Miri arrived. She looked fabulous in a dark blue dress and matching shoes. But there was something different about her…something hidden under lowered eyelids. Was she nervous? Miri could not remember ever seeing Dalia nervous.

"I'm glad you came," Dalia murmured, as if she had expected Miri to stand her up.

"So, we're back to the original plan?" Miri asked, once they had ordered drinks. "Convincing Seth to put the drawing on the legitimate market?"

"Yes—and the new information I have will make that easier." Dalia smiled.

Miri studied the menu. Her intention to order the most expensive item was already evaporating. The truth was that she was happy to be together with Dalia again. Still, whatever had overtaken her cousin on Saturday had given Miri two unhappy days. She ordered the second-most expensive item on the menu. Dalia smiled a twisted little smile but said nothing. She rubbed her right thumb back and forth along the length of her ring finger.

"You know, I don't think you realize how much I envy you," she said quietly.

Miri raised her eyebrows. This was an unexpected opening.

"Why would *you* envy *me*?"

"You're doing what you dreamed of."

Miri made a *pffft* sound with her lips. "Haven't I complained enough about my crummy job? I make next to nothing. I have to deal with my dad's constant pressure to get a 'reliable' job because I need his help with the rent. You envy *that*?"

"Things will get better for you. You're going to make it," Dalia said.

"Not if you and Seth drag me into a black-market sale."

"Seth is in a spot of trouble. He needs money. I can see that. We'll have to work on him. But I'm not on his side anymore."

She sounded sincere.

"OK, I was tempted by quick money," Dalia went on. "But what I found out changes that."

"But why would you *envy* me?" Miri persisted. "You have a good job. You help clients who need you."

Dalia began poking the cocktail stirrer into the lime wedge at the bottom of her glass.

"I don't really know why I went to law school," she said, more to herself than to Miri. "I guess it was because that's what Mom wanted me to do. She was a teacher, and she loved it, but after Vietnam, dad could never hold a job for long so she took a promotion to principal that she wasn't prepared for. She wanted to be sure I was prepared for a good job. I chose law. But being a lawyer just drains my soul. You think my clients need me? Maybe they do, for a day or two. I get them out of trouble and then the next week they get arrested again. It just goes around and around. I'm not really helping them. Not most of them, anyway. I'm just a temporary fix."

Miri had never heard her cousin talk like this. It made her nervous.

"But you do get paid pretty well," she said, trying to shift the mood back to a positive tone. "I love that dress. It's fabulous on you. You're so snatched."

Dalia flinched, as if the compliment had hit a nerve.

"Thanks. But I can't afford this dress."

Miri snorted. "Oh, sure."

Dalia only stared into her cocktail glass.

"I have a problem with money," she said finally. She spoke softly, not raising her eyes from her glass. A crease pulled her penciled eyebrows together. "That's what I need to explain to you. It's why I jumped at doing a deal with Seth. I saw a way to pay some of it off — not completely, but partly. Then I talked with my…"

"Whoa, whoa. Money problem? Pay some of *'it'* off? What are you talking about?"

"I'm talking about debt, Miri. I'm in debt, big time." Dalia attacked the lime wedge murderously with the cocktail stirrer. "Can't stop myself from buying things. I see a therapist. But..."

Her lips trembled. She kept her eyes fixed on the ice in her glass.

"I'm sorry about Saturday," she said. Her throat began to sound clogged. "You want to do the right thing with the O'Keeffe—get it authenticated and then whatever—sell it to a collector or give it to a museum. I respect that. I know: selling it on the black market is wrong. I just saw a way out of my problem and I jumped at it. You mean a lot to me. Your opinion of me means a lot. But the truth is, your opinion is much too high." A tear slid out from underneath one eyelash.

"No, it isn't," Miri said. Her voice sounded weaker than she wanted it to. Actually, she didn't know what to think. Did this explain Dalia's offer to help Seth sell the drawing on the black market? The Dalia she thought she knew wouldn't have done that.

The waiter arrived with a plate of salad in each hand. In a moment he returned with a small box of tissues.

Miri's mind was jumping around from one possibility to the next, trying out different visions of this new Dalia, the real Dalia. This Dalia was imperfect, damaged, unhappy. The big sister to whom Miri had confided all her frustrations was miserable herself.

"But between you and Josh, you must have plenty of money," Miri said slowly. "I mean, he's helping you out of this, right?"

Dalia reached for her glass. She speared the mangled piece of fruit with the cocktail stirrer, tossed it onto her salad plate, and sucked down the small amount of liquid that was left.

"Josh and I are in marriage counseling. He's been living with a friend."

"Josh moved out? Since when?"

"A couple of months." Now Dalia was poking at what was left of the lime wedge.

Miri reached over and plucked the cocktail stirrer out of her hand.

"You didn't say anything about that, either!" She tried to keep her voice soft, but she heard the sharp tone underneath. She bit the inside of her lip. "Well, I'm paying for this dinner."

"No, you're not. I invited you."

"But I picked the place. I picked Dazzled because it's expensive and I was mad at you."

"I know. Maybe you still are." Her cousin sat back in her chair with her hands in her lap. She huffed out a full breath. "At least now you know. You know everything."

Their voices had risen. Miri saw the couple at the next table turning to look at them.

Embarrassed, she said in a lower voice, "I don't know this new piece of information that you have. The blockbuster thing."

Dalia sat up and squared her shoulders.

"Ah! Thank you for rescuing our dinner from my problems," she said, lowering her own voice, too. "Listen. This will completely amaze you." There were still a few signs of tears on her face, but now her eyes were full of suppressed excitement. "So, I started wondering about that house that Seth is tearing down in Battle Hill. The little old house that had been owned by an old lady who was suing the present owner because he'd disposed of her heirloom sewing machine. The house with the Georgia O'Keeffe drawing hidden in the attic. Why was I curious? Because it's on *Marsh Street*. I know Marsh Street. You know how I know it?"

Miri raised her eyebrows. "No." She wondered if Dalia was pretending to be so excited in order to distract her from the confessions she'd made. But she didn't think so.

"Because," Dalia went on, "our great-grandparents' first house, when they moved to Battle Hill from the Lower East Side, was on Marsh Street. That place comes up in Aunt Rina's stories all the time. She lived there until she was seven or eight and she inherited it when our great-grandfather died. She only sold it last year."

Miri drew back her head and squinted at Dalia. "Aunt Rina? What? Wait…you think she has something to do with the O'Keeffe? That's crazy."

"Crazy, wild, unbelievable. All of that. But Seth said he's tearing down a house at 32 Marsh Street. I looked up the address in the 1920 Battle Hill city directory, online. Look!" Dalia pulled a folded piece of paper out of her purse. It was a printed screenshot of a page from the directory. She pointed to a line of tiny print and read it aloud: "32 Marsh Street. Mr. and Mrs. Solomon Lefkowitz."

Chapter 11

November 1909

It was a Friday night in November. The Sabbath feast was in the warming oven above the stove top. Mouthwatering smells of stuffed fish, chicken soup, roasted hen, a noodle kugel *and* a cabbage kugel filled the apartment. A beautiful, braided loaf of challah from the bakery sat on the table along with covered serving dishes holding pickled beets and garlicky green beans. Candles stood in tall silver candlesticks, ready to be lit at the moment of sundown.

Everything was prepared except the people. Matya and Avram were still dressing in the bedroom. Bennie and Bernie, Sol's half-brothers, were playing slapsies on the bed they shared, which was wedged into the kitchen next to the coal stove. In the apartment's third room, the parlor, Sol sat huddled on the sofa that was also his bed. A cold wind rattled the closed window; the wintery sound matched his bleak thoughts.

There was a knock at the apartment door.

"Bennie, open the door and let your big sister in," Matya called from the bedroom.

"Why can't she open it herself?" Bennie asked. Neither brother made a move to leave the overheated space next to the stove.

Another knock.

"Sol, please! Let them in."

Sol sighed. If only it were Rose on the other side of the door. He'd had only one more date with Rose since their walk in Central Park. On their first date, she had allowed him to kiss her lips. Twice. Two weeks later, on their second date, she had only allowed him to kiss her cheek. He had not heard from her in a month. The longing in his heart had grown dull and heavy.

He crossed the kitchen and opened the apartment door.

"Sol!" Mendel reached his hand out. "*Gut shabbos*. I was very glad to hear that you found a job."

"Yes. Thank you." Sol shook the offered hand warmly and returned the traditional Sabbath greeting, "*Gut shabbos*, Mendel. *Gut shabbos*, Hanna." Tonight was the first Sabbath dinner Mendel and Hanna had come to since his failure at working for them. Sol told himself firmly that he was past feeling bad about that.

Hanna gave him a tired smile and offered her cheek for a kiss.

That reminded Sol of Rose again and a pang of sadness went through him. He pressed his cheek against Hanna's quickly and said, "Here, give me your coats!"

"Where are you working?" Mendel asked kindly.

"Feldman's Clothing, for three weeks, now."

"I started at Greenbaum's Shirtwaists," Hanna told him.

"Congratulations," Sol said slowly. Talk of a general strike had been in the air for a couple of months. Workers had already struck at a few companies, mainly female workers who sewed women's clothing. *Shirtwaists,* he thought. *The center of the storm.* "How long have you been there? How is it?"

"Two weeks. It's OK. I just sew the same straight seam, over and over. I'm only a 'learner,' of course, so I don't even get regular pay yet."

Sol nodded. *Learner. Even worse.* The night Izzy had pulled him into the union meeting, he'd heard a woman protesting about being stuck as a learner. That was the lowest-pay category for sewers at many factories, especially for young women when they first started working. Once they were in that category, it was very difficult for them to 'graduate,' to regular pay.

"Come in. Sit near the stove. Bernie, could you move, please?" Sol hung the coats on the wall hooks.

He had not been hired as a learner. That was partly because he wasn't female, but also because he'd gotten some good advice. Yitzhak, the young redheaded fellow who had loaned Sol the last penny he'd needed outside Rivka's coffee house, had convinced him to take the electric sewing machine training class at Educational Alliance. So in September, Sol had stopped applying for jobs and enrolled. He discovered that most of the skills he'd learned on Matya's treadle machine transferred to an electric machine. After only three weeks, the instructor had written him a letter of recommendation and Sol went straight to work at Feldman's sewing sleeve and pant seams on men's casual suits. He had joined a union, of course, the Cloak and Suit Tailors Union, Local 9; his father had seen to that. The job was boring and repetitive. Still, he earned a lot more than he'd earned in the home factory doing Matya's job, enough to help the family buy food and pay a decent share of the rent. He felt bad that Hanna hadn't had the same advice.

"Hanna-le! Mendel!" Avram cried, emerging from the bedroom. "Did I hear that you're working, Daughter?"

Sol noticed tension sweep quickly across Mendel's face and realized that Hanna must have gone to work because the cap business was doing poorly, and they needed the money right away. So she'd *had* to begin as a learner; she wouldn't have had time to take the electric sewing machine class. Their desperation meant that she likely made about four dollars per week less than he did.

Hanna told Avram the news she'd told Sol.

Avram's mouth twisted with concern. "Shirtwaist? Hanna. You know a general strike will be called any day!"

Sol heard the energy rising in his father's voice. He knew what was coming—a bitter speech about the pay and conditions in the garment factories. Matya undoubtedly knew, too.

She bustled from the bedroom, clapping her hands. "Come on, everyone! It's time to light the candles!"

Matya was dressed in her Sabbath clothes, a dark blue dress with Russian lace around the neck and down the front. Like other very religious women, she wore the old-fashioned, dark brown wig she had brought from the old country over her own blond hair.

She struck a match. The family came to attention and watched as she lit the two candles in their polished silver candlesticks. Next, she waved her hands three times around the flames. Covering her eyes, she recited the blessing that brought the Sabbath to their household. Together, they all sang *Shalom Aleichem*—Peace Be With You—the ancient song that welcomed a visit from the Sabbath angels.

Sol wished that he could feel the Sabbath peace surround him. He needed it to overcome the six days of tension in his shoulders brought on by the always-renewing pile of cloth pieces to sew, and underneath that, his longing for Rose.

The flames of the two candles that Matya had just lit stretched upward bravely, like twin swords, offering hope and protection. Then something in the candles, or perhaps a draft from the leaky window, set the flames sputtering, shrinking, exploding sideways. No, his heart was not at peace; his life was too confusing.

ooo

Monday morning, Avram still had not received any word of a decision about a strike.

"So I should go to work?" Sol asked.

Avram shrugged. "Until you hear different."

On his way to Feldman's, Sol noticed far more people on the street than usual. Everyone was exchanging questioning looks, but no one offered any news. However, as he approached the factory, handwritten notes began to appear on walls and lamp posts. *Strike Information, 8:00 Sedalski's Deli, Everyone Welcome,* one said. *Join ILGWU!* said another.

Feldman's factory was unusually quiet. Taking his place at his sewing machine, he scanned the large room. A number of workers were absent, including the two women who usually sat on each side of him. Were the missing people out in the street, already part of the rising excitement?

At lunch break, Sol took his cheese and bread outside. Now the crowds were thicker. People stood in groups looking expectant. New signs had appeared on walls and lampposts. These all said the same thing: *General Meeting, Local 25, 6:30 p.m., Cooper Union Great Hall.*

Even fewer workers sat at machines in the workshop when he returned to Feldman's after lunch. By 3:30, only a dozen or so workers were left. Sol could just see the shoulder of the floor manager through the glass window in his office door. Even that shoulder looked tense. He grabbed his jacket and escaped.

Outside, sunset was only an hour away; the light was already starting to dim. But the sound of voices had grown louder.

Speakers stood on boxes or carts before groups of listeners. Their message was simple: *There is only one way for conditions and pay to improve. We must use the power of our numbers. Stand together! Strike!*

Glancing around, Sol noticed a thin young woman standing next to a lamppost on the other side of the street. She leaned forward towards the speaker, her face tilted up, her rapt expression lit by the low, orange light of late afternoon. A slight breeze lifted golden strands of her hair as well as pale tassels from the shawl she clutched around her. For a moment, Sol had the illusion that the shawl was actually a pair of feathered wings and that she might be some sort of spirit. Then with a small jolt, he recognized her. This was the woman he'd seen at Mendel's and Hanna's apartment on the day Mendel had had to fire him.

Just then, the crowd broke up into a hundred bodies all moving in different directions. When he got another view of the lamppost where the woman had been standing, she had vanished.

ooo

It was not even five o'clock, but thousands of people filled Seventh Street, all moving north. Sol fell in with the crowd. Their progress slowed two blocks from Cooper Union College and in another half block it came to a standstill. He heard that the great hall was full. There was a rumor that other lecture halls would be opened. But half an hour went by, night came, and Sol still stood in the same spot.

And yet, in every voice around him and in every glance, every smile between strangers, he felt excitement and hope. *This time change will come! We will make it happen!* A kind of light-headed drunkenness took hold of him.

Someone slapped his shoulder.

"Look who's here! Hello, Working Man!" It was Izzy. "You haven't been to class in weeks! How are you?"

"Good, I'm good! What's going on? What have you heard?"

"Nothing, yet. The meeting won't even start for an hour. And I wouldn't be surprised if it went on all night. The women are all pushing for a strike, but the men have doubts. That's why we're here. We'll convince them!" Izzy almost danced with determination.

"The numbers ought to convince them," Sol objected. He thought of Feldman's workshop, where there were four or five women to every man. The women paid their union dues even though they didn't make as much money as the men. He thought of Hanna. "Support the women!" he said loudly.

"Support the women!" Izzy echoed. He blew into his hands to warm them. "Speaking of women, I saw your rich girlfriend over at the Triangle Shirtwaist Factory this afternoon."

Sol's heart thudded. "Rose? …Where?"

"Triangle Shirtwaist. She was bringing coffee to the women marching on the picket line. She and her friends, the other *besere klas* ladies. She said she's been coming on Mondays since the women at Triangle went on strike." Izzy took note of Sol's stunned expression. "You didn't know. Ah." He patted Sol's arm. "Sorry, friend."

The darkness seemed to deepen suddenly. Or was it just despair?

Rose was here, downtown. He wanted to rush right over to the Triangle factory to see her. Why hadn't she left him a note at Rivka's coffee shop? Why didn't she want to see him? She had liked him; she had kissed him. She had filled his dreams. What had he done to turn her away?

"I'll bet her papa doesn't know where she goes on Mondays," Izzy said, half to himself.

Izzy's words were like the numbers that opened the kind of safe he'd seen in Mr. Koestlic's office ... *click* ... *click* ... *click*... clank....The heavy door swung open and let out a rush of thoughts.

Rose was here with the *"besere klas* ladies" — the uptown, upper class, wealthy society women who helped the striking women by contributing bail money and coffee. It was good of her to help his people...*his people*. Were his people different from her people? Rose had said they were not. *We've just been here a couple of generations longer*, she'd said.

Did that mean that his grandchildren, if he ever had any, would be like Rose? He couldn't imagine it.

What had given him the idea that he and Rose were equals? His friends who had seen them together must have thought that he planned to jump from the Lower East Side straight to the Koestlic's mansion, wherever it was. He blushed to think of that.

"I'm sure he doesn't know where she goes," Sol said. "She doesn't tell him. Her papa doesn't approve of her plans for her life."

"Oh? What does he think about the people she keeps company with?" Izzy asked.

"Me, you mean?"

But Izzy had turned to a group of young women standing in front of them. "Do you ladies know who is going to speak at the meeting?"

"Samuel Gompers," a serious-looking one said. Her voice held respect for the labor union leader, but at the same time it lacked enthusiasm. "It looks like the speakers are all men, and *they* don't want us women to strike. They think that our voices don't count. But I don't think even a third of the workers are men."

Her livelier friend put in, "Who runs the union? Men! But look at who's out here in the street. Women! Yet they claim if *we* struck it wouldn't change anything!"

"I've heard that," Izzy said. "And I say, shame on them! We're all in this together!"

"I love you!" the lively young woman cried. "Did you hear what he said? This man is on our side! What's your name? Why don't you go in there and tell those union men a thing or two? Oh, I wish you would!"

Izzy threw his hands up. "The hall has been full for more than an hour. They're not letting anyone else in."

"It's rotten," the young woman agreed. "All we can do is stand here and hope that lightning strikes them. But, oh! It was good to be out in the daytime, not sitting over that sewing machine!"

"This is not a picnic, Sadie," another young woman scolded.

"Don't I know it!" Sadie said. "Just remember that you're talking to a woman who clocks sixty-six hours every week. And can I make enough to live on?…As if there were any time left over to live."

"My sister just started as a learner," Sol said.

"Oh! That learner system! It stinks!" Sadie rolled her eyes.

"Yes, it's an abomination," the serious woman said. Her name was Esther. She asked where Hanna worked and if she was in the crowd. Sol was sure that Mendel would not have let Hanna come, but he didn't want to say so in front of these women.

Time passed. The clock on one of the college buildings said 9:30 and the messages coming out of the great hall still did not mention a strike. The speeches were about typical pro-union topics like worker solidarity, but nothing about the issue they were all there for.

"They're trying to fill up the time until everyone's so tired they just go home!" Esther said. "Look around. The crowd is already thinner."

"They're going to have to vote soon," Izzy said.

"If they don't declare a strike tonight, I'll have to be at work at 7 o'clock tomorrow morning," said a young man behind them. "I've got to get to bed."

Sol and the women turned.

"Well, I'm not leaving," Sadie said. "I'm here to the end, and it better end with a vote to strike!"

For a second, the young man looked sheepish. But then he tipped his hat and departed.

Sol had begun to think about leaving, too, but Sadie's words gave him new strength. Esther was right, though. In the next half hour, they moved up more than a block as people in front of them left. A few women even came out of the door. One was in tears. Her friend, a tall, angry-looking woman perhaps in her thirties, steered the crying woman through the crowd.

"So? Nothing?" Sadie asked the friend as they passed.

"It's like all those people are hypnotized!" the tall woman snapped. "Makes me want to scream. Someone needs to wake them up!"

They were close enough to the door by that time to hear the applause as another speech ended. Forty or fifty people came barging out, taking great gulps of fresh air and not meeting anyone's eyes.

"Come on!" Sadie said. She grabbed Izzy's arm with one hand and Esther's with the other. Izzy grabbed Sol. They rushed inside.

ooo

The only light in the huge hall came from the stage. Sol, being pulled along by Izzy, had an impression of arches and columns, but he hardly understood the space he was in. He knew only that the Great Hall was in the basement of the Cooper Union College building and that it was packed with people way past its capacity. If there had been any empty seats, people standing against the walls had taken them before Sol and his group even got through the door. He and Izzy burrowed in among the mass of standing bodies.

The air smelled foul, and although it was dark, it was not quiet. Well over a thousand people shifted restlessly in their seats or shuffled their feet. The vast room was filled with an impatient, complaining buzz. Two women and a man sitting at the ends of rows near Sol slumped in their seats looking dazed by exhaustion or perhaps by the lack of oxygen. On the stage, a man in a suit had apparently just begun a speech.

Sol heard, "…plot our steps carefully and weigh each consequence…."

"What's going on?" he asked the woman standing next to him. She must have been in the meeting for some time; the sleeves of her blouse were rolled up, her celluloid collar was loosened, and her round-lensed eyeglasses rode crookedly on her nose.

"Gompers finally spoke just now. He's against a strike, wouldn't you know?" she said bitterly. "This guy is his sidekick." She made a disgusted growl. "What a bosher parade! We should all walk out!"

Just then, there was a disturbance near the stage.

"Let me speak!" came a clear woman's voice.

A chorus of female voices took up the cry. "Let her speak!" "She wants to speak!"

Sol craned his neck. A knot of people, women and men, had formed in front of the stage. They half-lifted, half-pushed a slim young woman up into the light. She found her balance and stepped towards the lectern in a determined way. Energy radiated from her straight eyebrows and direct gaze. The man who had been speaking gave way.

"It's Clara!" said the woman next to Sol, straightening her eyeglasses. 'Oh, *good*!"

The woman on the stage was already speaking. "I am Clara Lemlich," she said in a ringing voice. "I have listened to all the speakers, and I have no further patience for talk!"

She spoke in a Ukrainian dialect of Yiddish. Sol understood her perfectly, but a cry of "Translation!" arose. Of course, some of the workers were Italian or other nationalities. Here and there, voices began to repeat Lemlich's words in English, so that Sol heard her speech in two languages and many versions:

"I am a working girl, one of those who are on strike against intolerable conditions. I am tired of listening to speakers who talk in general terms. What we are here for is to decide whether we shall strike or shall not strike. I offer a resolution that a general strike be declared—now!"

The sleepy, restless audience took a collective breath and woke up with a roar. Instantly united, they stamped their feet, waved handkerchiefs.

It took a long time for the chairman of the meeting to call them back to order. But when there was near-quiet, he asked for a second to Lemlich's resolution. The whole audience shouted its second. The chairman had the lights turned on and called for the vote.

Sol did not see a single person who didn't have at least one hand in the air. Despite the doubts of the union leaders, the general strike was on!

ooo

The hours chatting with Sadie and Esther and the others during the strike meeting had temporarily soothed the sting of Rose's indifference. *There are other young women,* Sol had thought to himself. If he'd been talking with Esther without her friends around, he might have asked her to have coffee with him. But during the long walk home, loneliness repossessed him. Rose had approached him, singled him out as special in her eyes, excited his longing for her. Why had she then rejected him?

He arrived in low spirits. Matya was waiting for him

"I spoke with the *shadkhanit* today, Sol. He says he has just the woman for you."

"What? I said no to that," Sol said impatiently.

Matya didn't answer him directly.

"You have a job, and now you will have a good Jewish wife to make a home with," she said. "This is the best thing for you, Sol, believe me."

Thoughts, some despairing, some resigned, twisted through Sol's mind like a storm of snowflakes. *Who I make a home with is mine to choose. I wanted Rose.*

But after all, who am I? I am part of the group that was out there on the street, the group who is exploited. Rose is on the other side. I would be betraying my people, my place in history, to be with her.

And underneath it all, the hard, icy truth: and anyway, what does it matter? She doesn't want me.

"Oh, all right," he said roughly. "What's the use?" He told himself that whatever he said right now didn't matter. The strike was what mattered, and it was in the way of everything else. He couldn't possibly get married without some savings to set up a home and now he would be out of work for who knew how long? He was too exhausted, too full of anticipation for the picket line. Who could take the idea of marriage seriously?

Chapter 12
2009

Marsh Street was not on the hill that Battle Hill was named for. It was in a flat area that had once been a swamp. Small, uncared-for houses lined the street. In the 1890s, building them was a popular investment for middle-class people in the town. The investors rented them to workers at a large furniture factory that had just opened. By 1920, though, the original builders had grown old and lost interest in maintaining the properties. One by one, they were sold to young couples who were just starting out in life.

Ninety years passed. The little houses on Marsh Street sagged. Their paint peeled. Plastic tarps covered leaking roofs. Apparently they weren't worth fixing anymore, and one by one, the little houses were torn down.

Miri and Dalia stood on the sidewalk in front of 32 Marsh Street. All that was left of the roof were the bare rafters. The shingles that had covered the rafters, plus insulation, were heaped in a corner of the yard.

"Might as well take a picture of it anyway," Dalia said, holding up her phone.

"A picture of the actual spot where the drawing was, inside the insulation, would have been a good piece of evidence," Miri said, disappointed.

It was Saturday and the site was deserted. They heard the sound of shoes meeting a soccer ball. Far down the street, two boys practiced their passing, working around the potholes in the pavement. Dalia snapped a few photos of the house and turned away.

"Ready to go?" she asked.

Miri still stood, looking. "Our great grandparents actually lived here?"

"Absolutely. From 1920 to 1930 or so. Grandpa and Rina were born in this house."

"How do you know all that?"

"How? Did you forget that I grew up just down the road in Southport? We used to come over to Battle Hill all the time. Grandpa and Great Aunt Rina liked to tell stories about the old days."

"I don't remember that."

"You and your mother only came east for Passover. When Grandma died, you were only…what? Seven?"

"Eight."

One year ago, when Miri moved to New York for graduate school, Dalia had brought her to visit Rina. Rina had told her stories about Miri's mother Lilian as a child. It hadn't occurred to Miri then that Rina was also a link to *her* mother, Miri's great-grandmother. Ilka? Elka? Something like that. She'd never thought about her great-grandmother.

"I was fifteen," said Dahlia. "I went to a lot more seders than you did."

"They weren't here, though, were they? I remember a big house."

"That was the house they moved to after this one. When Grandpa was eleven."

This sudden view into her family's past seized Miri.

"So, have you been to this house before?"

Dalia shrugged. "We've driven past it. I've never been inside. There were always renters."

"Well, it won't be here much longer," Miri said. "Let's check it out." She crossed the short front walk and climbed the plywood ramp, where the front steps had been.

"Really?" Dalia, of course, was dressed in a pale green summer dress and open sandals with little heels.

Miri ignored the "No Trespassing, Construction Zone" sign and pushed open the battered front door. Her running shoes crunched on scraps of wood and bent nails as she stepped inside. Slowly, her eyes adjusted and walls painted a dark salmon color came into view. She peeked into the empty kitchen. Its bare walls had wide, unpainted stripes where cabinets had hung. A sour smell drifted up from torn layers of floor covering.

And yet, standing still, there in the middle of what might have been the dining area, she let her mind fill the rooms with a table and chairs, an old-fashioned sofa, a book case in the corner. Dim, shadowy people, many people through many years, inhabited the space.

"Uff!" Dalia said, finally entering the door. "This probably isn't safe. And if anyone catches us in here, we'll be in trouble."

Miri hardly heard her. Lost in her imagination, she passed through the kitchen to a hallway. A square hole in the ceiling must have been where folding, pull-down attic stairs had been. She would have gone up, but there was no ladder nearby. Anyway, the attic was gone. All she saw through the hole was blue sky and a few clouds behind the roof framing.

"That's where the drawing was?"

"That's what Seth said," Dalia answered. "Also, an old treadle sewing machine that belonged to our great-*great* grandmother.   Great-great-*step*-grandmother.   Great-Aunt Rina is suing Seth's boss because she put in the sale contract that she had the right to the sewing machine, and he sold it."

Miri peeked into the three doors off the hallway. The first had been a bathroom. The other two, one on either side of the passage, were bedrooms.

"How many kids were there?" she asked aloud.

"Three," Dalia said from the kitchen. "Well, actually, four. The first boy died in the 1918 flu epidemic. Then Ruth, Morris, and Rina."

"Ruth? Grandpa had a sister Ruth?"

"Uh-huh. She married an Italian man and converted. Died in the 1960s."

"Mom never told me that."

"They didn't speak of her after she married a Catholic. But yes, she was Grandpa's older sister."

"So, where did the kids sleep?" Miri asked.

"In the big bedroom, I guess. Grandpa said they hung a curtain across the room between him and the two girls." Dalia picked her way through lumps of broken plaster on the floor and went into the larger bedroom. "Yes! Look— there's still a piece of wood attached to the ceiling! I'll bet that's what they hung the curtain from."

The one-by-two-inch strip of wood had been painted over so many times that it seemed to be part of the ceiling. Miri stared at it. Chills ran down the backs of her arms. This narrow piece of wood connected her to a relative she'd never thought about before: her great-grandfather Solomon Lefkowitz had lived in this very house.

Miri turned to Dalia, questions about their great-grandfather on her lips.

But Dalia had already left the bedroom. "Let's go, Miri," she said briskly from the hallway. "We have other business to take care of."

ooo

Miri had pictured Seth living in an apartment in the basement of an old house. But Dalia parked in front of a modern concrete building on a downtown street. The two stores on the building's street level sold baby clothes and arts and crafts materials. Stairs to the second floor were behind a door with a keypad lock. Next to the door were four buttons. "S. Lefkowitz" was printed on a fresh slip of paper next to the first button. The labels next to the second and third buttons were grey and faded, but the fourth button also had a fresh label, only with a female name.

"Hm," Dalia said.

She pushed the button next to Seth's name.

After a minute, she pushed it again and held it for a longer time.

A speaker crackled. "Who is this?" Seth's voice demanded.

"Your neighbor," Dalia said. "I left the door code upstairs. Can you let me in?"

There was a ten second hesitation. Then the lock clicked. Dalia quickly pulled the door open. Their steps echoed as they climbed concrete stairs.

"Why did you do that?" Miri whispered.

Dalia stopped climbing. "I don't know. You're right, there wasn't any point to it." She thought for a moment, then shook her head. "This is the kind of thing I have to do for my job. I used to think it was fun, but it's twisted my mind."

The hall at the top of the stairs had openings in the brick walls that let in some daylight and outside air. Four doors, two on each side of the hall, had apartment numbers. Dalia knocked on the yellow metal door with the number 1 on it.

Footsteps. Miri felt Seth peering through the peep hole. The door snapped open.

"What the hell?"

"Sorry. Thought you might not let us in," Dalia said. "We need to talk to you."

"Well, I would have," Seth said. "I need to talk to *you*." He stood back and let them enter.

If the building was not where Miri had imagined Seth would live, his apartment was even more of a surprise. She had expected an unmade bed, dirty carpet, dust everywhere. Instead, it was as neat as a pin.

Seth sat on the bed, leaving the two chairs that went with the small table for Miri and Dalia.

"So?" he said.

"So, we stopped over to the house at 32 Marsh," Dalia said.

"What for?"

Miri responded with a question. "Did you happen to snap any pics of the drawing where you found it? In place, before you pulled it out?"

Seth snorted. "You still want evidence that I'm telling the truth?"

"No. I was hoping for evidence to help with authentication. Like, maybe, a picture showing the shape of the frame impressed into the insulation."

Seth pressed his lips together and his eyes flickered from her to Dalia. A chill ran down Miri's arms. She reminded herself that Seth was not Chuck. She had no reason to assume he'd be violent.

"I did take a couple of pictures after I pulled it out," he said. "I set it on the floor next to where I'd found it and photographed it there." He pulled his phone out of his pocket.

Miri held her breath.

"But it doesn't show what you want," he said. "I'd say that original insulation was installed in the 1920s. The stuff they used back then was crumbly. It had all sifted out the cracks in the boards. The drawing was just sitting in an empty space. There wasn't any impression."

The pictures he showed them were useless.

Once again, Miri saw a look of caution on his face. He wasn't angry, but he *was* holding something back. What?

"Well, that's too bad," Dalia cut in. "We have some other news for you, though. Something that I think will change your mind about selling the drawing for fast cash."

"Hmph!" Seth said.

"Hmph…what?" Dalia asked. "What's on your mind, Seth?" Clearly, she was picking up the same vibes as Miri.

"Go on," Seth said. "Let's hear your news."

"That house was owned by our great-grandfather, Solomon Lefkowitz, and then by his daughter, Great-Aunt Rina," Dalia said. "So the drawing may legally belong to us."

Seth was clearly taken aback.

"Oh?" he said, half to himself. "That's weird." Then he searched Dalia's face. "Wait…*us*?

"Well, yes. Us. His descendants. Actually, Great-Aunt Rina would be first in line."

But at that moment, his phone, which was balanced on his knee, gave out a mournful ring tone—like a ship lost in fog. The skin around Seth's eyes tightened. He stood and walked out into the hall with the phone.

As the door closed, they heard him say, "Dad? What is it?"

Dalia raised an eyebrow. "Problem there," she said.

Miri recalled the conversation she'd had with Seth after she'd thrown Dalia out of her apartment. The tension between them had softened when he'd explained that he wanted to sell the O'Keeffe drawing to replace what he'd sold to pay the lawyer in Seattle. But in the week that followed, she'd wondered why her uncle had been so hard on Seth. Uncle Ira could have paid the lawyer, or at least loaned Seth the money.

The door opened and Seth came back in. His mouth was set in a line and his eyes were angry.

"That was your dad?" Miri asked.

"Yeah."

Miri took a risk. "I guess you're angry at him for making you sell your truck and your tools to pay the lawyer?" she said.

"He didn't make me," Seth said. "He would have paid. And then I would have been in his debt forever. I got myself into this hole, I'll get myself out."

Miri was silent. Seth's answer cast an entirely new light on why he was so set on selling the drawing. It wasn't just to replace his tools. He was trying to stand on his own two feet. Just like her. And it answered the question of what The System was—or whom. It was his dad.

"What were you saying?" he asked, wearily.

"I had just told you that the house you're tearing down was our great-grandfather's and the drawing you found might already belong to us," Dalia answered. "It gives us a lot more power, speeds up the whole process," she went on. "We can get the investigation going right away."

"The investigation is already under way," Seth said.

"What do you mean?" Miri said sharply.

"I mean I've gone ahead with the sale."

Miri's heart lurched as adrenalin shot through her arteries. She felt the O'Keeffe drawing flying out of her grasp. She hadn't imagined Seth would do this. She'd thought she understood him, but she hadn't.

"I've already met with Silverman, the lawyer you mentioned." Seth nodded at Dalia. "He's going to work both sides of the deal. He's finding someone to authenticate the drawing, and he has a client he's sure will buy it."

Miri let out a sound between a growl and a wail.

"No! What have you done? Where is it?" she demanded.

"In Rocky Silverman's safe."

Chapter 13
March 1911

Sol stood under the *huppah*, the wedding canopy, awaiting his bride. He wore a wedding *kittel*, a white robe, over his suit. Its whiteness was meant to show that he was starting this new stage of his life fresh and unstained. It had occurred to him that the *kittel* looked similar to a shroud.

Sol's father and two half-brothers stood by him. He had fasted all day, as was the custom, and he felt lightheaded. His body swayed; it wasn't unheard of for the bridegroom to faint. He hoped his father and brothers would catch him if that happened.

"Sol, please! Some joy on your wedding day!" Izzy was holding up one of the two front poles of the *huppah*. He murmured, but apparently not softly enough, because a woman in the front of the women's side of the sanctuary responded.

"Oh, the joy of the first year of marriage!" she exclaimed sentimentally. She was one of the Lefkowitz's neighbors.

"Happy wedding day!" called a woman dressed in a wine-colored machine-lace gown that was mended in only a few places. Another woman began to sing a Yiddish song about the joy of shining children's faces. The first woman joined in huskily. She twirled, clapping her hands above her head. The two danced around each other, bumping shoulders.

The first two parts of the ceremony were already finished. In his study, Rabbi Grinstein had read the standard wedding contract to Sol, and Sol had agreed to it. Next, he had been escorted to the bride's receiving room, where he had to look into her face and confirm that, yes, this woman was his intended wife. Only, his throat had locked up and he had merely nodded. Then he had placed the crown on her head so that the veil attached to it completely screened her face.

Sol and Ilka had been engaged for sixteen months. Her family consisted of one older brother in Ohio, her cousin Mendel, who was Sol's brother-in-law, and Mendel's widowed mother, Ilka's aunt. Her parents and younger sisters hadn't made it to America.

Supposedly, she and Sol had come to know each other at their meetings. They met at his parents' apartment, at her aunt's, or more often at Hanna and Mendel's. But a male chaperone always had to be present, which froze their words and feelings.

They did have one thing in common. They had both supported the shirtwaist makers' strike, as well as the cloakmaker's strike that had followed it the next summer. The bitterly fought shirtwaist maker's strike, known by now as the Uprising of the 20,000, lasted for eleven violent weeks. Almost three out of four of the strikers were women, but that didn't stop the police from breaking strikers' ribs and throwing them in jail. The Uprising of the 20,000 won only some of the strikers' demands, but the two strikes together were the beginning of big changes in the "needle trades." So Sol and Ilka had that to talk about.

But Ilka had not had the opportunity for much education. Although she listened closely to Sol's ideas when he offered them, she rarely asked a question. He would have thought that she was dull except for the flashes of understanding in her eyes and the tension in her body. After all that time, Ilka was still a mystery to him; he suspected there was more to her than she showed him, but he had no clue about what that might be. To be fair, he supposed she could have said almost the same thing about him.

Those months were a dark time for Sol. The dreams he had brought with him to America were dying. It had been obvious from his arrival that America was not the magic place that people in the Russian Pale had said it was. But he'd still had hope. Sitting on a hard bench stitching sleeves for ten hours a day, though, he had come to know that the life of his dreams was unreachable.

ooo

Footsteps sounded on the wooden floor behind the door to the synagogue's small sanctuary. The door opened with a little whine that twanged Sol's nerves.

The cantor broke into a song for the bridal procession. Blinded by the veil, Ilka Kalinski was led into the sanctuary by her aunt and her about-to-be mother-in-law, Matya.

The rest went quickly.

The bride, obviously navigating by her view of Sol's shoes, circled him seven times. Her aunt then helped her find her station at Sol's right side. Izzy handed a plain gold ring to Sol who, speaking the required words, placed it on Ilka's slim forefinger. Finally, Rabbi Grinstein spoke the seven blessings that married them. Then he filled the wine glass, blessing that, too.

The wine went straight to Sol's head. He raised Ilka's veil and held the glass to her lips. Their eyes met; her brown-eyed gaze was startlingly direct.

As the rabbi wrapped the empty wineglass in a napkin and placed it on the floor next to Sol's foot, the cantor began to chant "If I Forget Thee, O Jerusalem," Psalm 137 from the Bible. The words lamented the Jewish exile to Babylonia almost 3,000 years before. It never failed to bring the older immigrants to tears. Usually, they succeeded in feeling optimistic about their new lives in America. But the plaintive tune brought memories of the 'old country' that they, too, had been forced by violence to leave.

Sol usually scoffed at this sentimentalism, this confusion of the biblical story with the reality of living people. But today as he raised his foot to stamp on the wineglass, his own sentimental feelings possessed him and tugged his heart down. It seemed to him that the wineglass symbolized his youth and all his young hopes.

"*Don't* remember," he told himself. He was a married man now. He had a wife to feed and clothe, and perhaps he'd have children to support in the future. He had to forget his last shreds of hope of studying psychology, had to break the last, thin, thread of memory still attaching him to Rose.

With a sob, he smashed his foot down, hard.

The guests exploded into celebration.

"*Mazel tov!* Congratulations! May you have a long and happy life together!" they shouted, clapping him on the shoulders. They wrung his hand, threw foil-wrapped chocolate kisses and paper confetti into the air. The musicians broke into a wild Eastern European tune that swiftly wove back and forth between joyous and heartbroken. Guests and family danced after the band up a flight of stairs to the banquet hall.

Sol and Ilka, however, were led away from the crowd to the rabbi's study for the last step in their marriage ceremony, the *yichud*. Here they would spend a few minutes together, alone for the first time as a married couple.

The door closed behind them. A mild terror seized Sol.

"Solomon," Ilka said. There was an urgent edge to her tone. He turned to her.

Determination, he read in her eyes. *And nervousness.* She started to say something, then took a breath and lowered her gaze.

"Shall we sit?" she said. "I'm hungry, aren't you?"

A dairy meal had been set out on a low table in front of a sofa. Sol sat, although he wasn't sure he could eat. Ilka's hand shook slightly as she poured coffee.

"Cream?" she asked calmly. Sol accepted. He tasted a glass of fruit juice. Orange: a luxury! One platter held three bagels and a small brick of cream cheese, a second held slices of pound cake and fruit compote. Ilka served him carefully.

They both nibbled.

Ilka had thrown her veil back from her face and he noticed now what he hadn't noticed when he'd put the veil in place—the effort that she had put into her appearance. Her cheeks glowed with rouge, and she had shaped her eyebrows into a fashionable arch. With her narrow face and slightly protruding front teeth, though, she was still plain.

In pulling the stiff veil completely off, she loosened a long strand of her blond hair from the bun on top of her head. Later she would take her hair down completely, Sol thought. He was ready for that—half alive to it and half resigned.

"Solomon…" During the entire sixteen months of their engagement, she had always called him by his full name.

"Sol," he said softly.

She swallowed. "Sol. We haven't talked freely, not the whole time that we've been engaged. I haven't. I couldn't, in front of my cousin and the others."

"Is there something…?"

"No, no, nothing that you don't know," she said, smoothing the skirt of her bridal gown with both hands. She looked up at him—again, that direct, brown-eyed gaze. "Only, how much I want to be able to tell you things!"

Prickles of caution raised the hairs on Sol's arms, but at the same time a sliver of relief, like a pinpoint of light, penetrated the fog of his feelings. Until today, much of his imagining of his future with Ilka had consisted of avoiding imagining it. But now, he had stepped into that future. It wouldn't be their engagement period anymore. Things would change; of course they would.

"I already know everything important about you," he said gently.

"Yes, maybe, but I want you to know…This is hard…."

"What is it, then?"

Suddenly, words began to pour out of her.

"…that I am glad that I am your wife, Sol. That I will work by your side, to make a good life with you. I want to say that you can trust me. You can rely on me. I will never let you down. I have wanted you to hear that!"

Sol stared, speechless. He had come to expect ordinary, everyday comments from Ilka, certainly not these noble ideas.

"Oh, I know," she said. "…at least, I think…that our marriage was not easy for you to accept. Not as easy as it was for me. But I want you to be happy. I promise you I will work to make our life a success."

The way she lifted her gaze to him made him remember the rapt expression on her face that he'd seen from across the crowd at the shirtwaist makers' strike. During the sixteen months since then, her control over her emotions had erased that memory. But here again, he saw the passion he had seen that evening. It had been there all along. For him.

Moved, he leaned forward and kissed her.

Her mouth tasted slightly of the onions on the bagels; her protruding front teeth were right behind her lips. It was nothing like Rose's teasing kisses that had so inflamed his fantasies. On the other hand, Ilka put her arms around him and pressed against him eagerly, surprisingly eagerly.

ooo

After they had eaten cake and fruit, they joined the wedding party on the second floor. If Ilka's parents had been there, they would have been responsible for the wedding dinner; however, they had been lost in the 1905 pogrom in Yekaterinoslav. In their place, the duty had fallen to Avram and Matya—but they could not afford a sit-down dinner for the forty people who were invited. The compromise was a buffet dinner with baskets for guests to contribute what they could plus a little extra to distribute to the poor.

The really orthodox European tradition forbid men and women from dancing together. However, this congregation was more American. Hanna had insisted that Avram hire the most popular group of musicians on the Lower East Side, the *Meshuganer Honner*, the Crazy Roosters.

The merrymaking was well underway when Sol and Ilka entered the banquet hall.

As soon as they appeared, the musicians began the Brides Waltz, a slow and graceful piece. The just-married couple had to dance alone once around the floor, in front of everyone. Matya had instructed Sol in this until he was adept at steering her around the parlor. Of course, he'd never practiced with Ilka, but he turned to her with his best imitation of confidence. To his surprise, Ilka showed no hesitation at all. She plucked up the wide skirt of her white gown with her right hand, raised her left hand towards his shoulder, and threw back her head with a smile. Sol's right hand found the center of her back, and they were off. How different it was to waltz with a slim, light-footed woman! They swept around the floor while everyone clapped and called out good wishes.

Next came polkas, *kadrils*, more waltzes, and a *freylakh*, in which a long line of dancers snaked around the room, each person dancing as he or she pleased. As the *freylakh* ended, a call came: "Chair dance! Chair dance!" Sol and Ilka were captured and raised up on chairs, like a king and queen. They each grasped opposite corners of a large handkerchief. Sol couldn't help laughing because Ilka was laughing and screaming as they were danced about on high. Both of them tried desperately to stay on their chairs, each pulling on the handkerchief when the other was in danger of sliding off.

When the music was over and their feet were on the floor, Ilka fell into his arms, weak with thrills and laughter.

But Sol had seen something from the chair as it tipped and spun—a splash of white near the stairway. Someone new had come into the hall. The presence of that person was like a ghost's touch. He turned and the breath went out of him.

Rose.

The music seemed to grow distant, and the floor felt unstable.

She was just slipping one arm out of a light grey coat with a white rabbit-skin collar. Under the coat, she wore a light blue, floor-length afternoon dress draped with a layer of matching lace. Catching his eye, she smiled, showing her perfect white teeth between lips painted the color of cherries.

He had never seen Rose dressed and made-up like this. The enormous gulf between his social level and hers was suddenly more clear to him than it had ever been.

"Who is that?" Ilka asked.

Sol realized that he still had one arm around her. He withdrew it quickly. His mind raced.

"That's...my boss's daughter," he lied. "He must have sent her to...to congratulate us. I'll speak to her."

"But...."

Sol was already moving toward Rose. His thoughts, which usually proceeded in a straight, logical manner, fluttered about like the confetti his friends had thrown at him. He felt that he, himself, was floating, tossed about in whirling currents of air. He had never expected to see Rose again except as the phantom of his imagination that she had become. And yet, here she was, in the flesh, on the very day that his fate without her—and without the more educated, free-thinking part of America that she came from—was sealed. She was, in some sense, his Jerusalem, the past from which he was exiled, the future he had dreamed of.

"Hello, Rose." He noticed that his heart, unlike his mind, was not fluttering. It was quiet, questioning.

"I'm probably intruding," Rose said. She didn't sound apologetic. "But I heard you were getting married today and I wanted to say congratulations in person. I know that I stopped seeing you rather…abruptly…." She almost ran out of breath at this point, as if she had been riding on a tippy chair instead of him. But then she tossed her head and opened her mouth to continue.

"Why did you?" Sol asked, before she could speak.

"Stop seeing you? Oh. Because I'm not looking for this." She tipped her head to indicate everything—the ceremony that had occurred and the celebration that was going on— marriage in total. "…But I enjoyed knowing you, Sol. Truly. And I want to give this to you, and to your wife, to show my good wishes."

For the first time Sol noticed that she was holding a flat, square, package.

His lips parted, but no words came out.

"It's just a small decoration for your new home. Something I found at the Art Students' League. I liked it and I like to support young artists. I wish you every success, Sol. I know you'll find it."

Her hazel eyes shifted focus then, to something behind him. Sol turned his head. Ilka was staring at Rose and him, her eyebrows raised as if she was waiting. A few other people had stopped talking or dancing and had begun to watch what was going on.

A moment passed, during which Sol realized that both Rose and Ilka expected him to introduce them to each other. He exhaled sharply. All his instincts were against that.

"Miss Koestlic!" Izzy's voice, relaxed and faintly amused, cut through the silence. "How nice to see you! Unexpected, but nice." Izzy stepped between Sol and Rose.

He took Rose's arm with one hand and swooped up her coat with the other. "May I have a word?"

Without a glance backward, Izzy steered her out to the stair landing. When he returned, he brought the square package with him.

"She insists that I give this to you," he told Sol privately. "I believe she's actually sincere. She doesn't mean any harm by showing up here; she just can't imagine that it might cause a problem. Whew! What a woman!"

"Keep that for me, please. I'll get it in a few days."

A week later, Sol brought the package home to his and Ilka's apartment. Inside was a framed drawing done in charcoal on pale parchment-colored paper. It was in the new, abstract style and it struck him immediately as full of meaning. Dark, angular forms weighted down the bottom, but larger, oval shapes, like sprouts swelling with life, burst out above the heaviness. And rising through it all, rippling lines suggested flowing water or folds of living tissue ready to unfurl.

Hope, he thought.

"It's beautiful." He tilted it so Ilka could see it.

She sniffed.

May 1914

"Ach! You young fellows have it easy!" Moishe Pinsky said. He was a little man, shaped like a bent stalk of ripe wheat. He grasped the messy stack of suit fabric laid out on the cutting table and flipped and rippled all thirty sheets of cloth into perfect order. "See how I did that?"

"No," Sol said.

"So next time, watch closely. It's all in the wrists."

"Next time, do it more slowly," Sol said.

"Ach, you can't do it slow. It don't work slow."

"Show me in the air," Sol demanded. "Let's see how your wrists move."

It was his first day on the cutting floor of the factory. He'd just been promoted to assistant cutter, a big step up, and after only four years at Feldman's Clothing! He and Ilka had been hoping for this. He knew that going back to work after little Yussel was born had been hard on her, even though she'd insisted. She'd wanted to put the extra money away. Now he would make twenty-one dollars a week and she could go down to part-time.

But Pinsky wasn't making his training easy.

"I don't know how to show you," he complained. "It's a knack. You got the knack or you don't, that's all."

"Are you telling me you were born knowing how to do that?" Sol asked.

"Maybe I was. It feels like it. Thirty-five years I've been doing this. OK, OK, next time I'll try to show you each move separately. You young guys gotta be spoon-fed."

"That's right. Would you give a baby a whole bowl of Cream of Wheat? He'd throw it all over the walls. Give him one spoon at a time, and he gets it down."

"Very clever!" Pinsky said. "I like that. Little baby. All right, now, we're going to lay out the pattern pieces. One. At. A. Time. Watch me."

They proceeded at a slower pace through the steps of laying out the wooden pattern pieces and drawing around them with chalk. Pinsky showed him how to hold the electric cutting tool, how to always watch where the cord was so he didn't cut through it. Guiding the cutter through all those layers of cloth while making clean, straight lines and curves was hard physical work after years of sitting at a sewing machine. But after Sol had cut out five stacks of pants legs, Pinsky grunted approval.

"You'll do all right," he said.

It was when Sol had finished cutting out all the pieces that the idea came to him.

Pinsky sliced up the remains of the fabric into smaller bits and tossed them into big canvas bins. There were eight bins heaped with multi-colored scraps of cloth, waiting for the bin-boy to wheel them away.

"That's a lot of waste fabric," Sol said.

"Yah. Lots of people have tried to find something to do with it," Pinsky said. "None of them worked out, so they're still sending it all to the dump. Come up with one that works, you could make yourself a millionaire. Ha, ha!"

Sol squinted at the bins. The colors blended together into a marbled mass. It reminded him of something he'd seen once before. Something on the floor in the window of a store.

A braided rag rug.

Chapter 14

2009

Rocky Silverman's office was in an older but still classy neighborhood near Central Park. On Monday morning, Miri called in to work to say she'd forgotten she had a doctor's appointment. She and Dalia rode the bus uptown. They were going to confront Silverman and demand the drawing back.

"Let me do the talking," Dalia said. "I know how he thinks." She didn't seem particularly worried. She knew Silverman from court cases and she thought he was full of hot air.

But dealing with Silverman felt dangerous to Miri.

"Are you sure we want to do this?" she asked.

Maybe there was some other way to get the drawing back. Why, oh why, had Seth decided to trust Silverman?

Dalia gave her a hard look. "I'm not sure that you'd be able to live with yourself if we didn't."

Miri sighed deeply and chewed on the inside of her mouth.

After they got off the bus, Dalia led them to a side street around the corner from an antiques store. The name

"Rocco Silverman, Attorney" was painted on the lower corner of the window in small black letters.

Inside, a slim young man with many piercings sat at the receptionists' desk. His orange and yellow hairstyle looked like wind-whipped fire. He wore a tank top and full sleeves of tattoos covered both arms.

Dalia nodded to him. "Is he on the phone?"

"No," the young man said, without taking his eyes off his computer screen.

Dalia did not wait to be announced or shown into Silverman's office. She pulled open a pair of heavy doors and entered.

As Miri followed, her eyes fell on a black and white lithograph hanging on the waiting room wall. An Ellen Volotny piece, she noted. How appropriate. Volotny was represented by a gallery with a shady reputation. If Silverman dealt with *them*....

Rocky Silverman's vast desk held only a small laptop computer. Behind him, a large marble statue of the Roman god Mercury crouched on a low cabinet. Mercury: the god of beautiful speech, wealth, and thieves.

Silverman was in his 50s. He wore a handsome, dark grey Italian suit and a thick, lavender silk tie. His long face ended in a strong chin. His skin radiated health. Seeing Dalia, he smiled, showing gleaming white teeth.

"Dolly!" he exclaimed, as if he was surprised and delighted. He stood.

Dalia reached out for a handshake. Silverman's other arm came around her and pulled her into a hug. They air-kissed.

"You look gorgeous, as usual," he said, sliding his eyes down her body. Dalia smiled briefly and smoothed her slinky knit dress. Miri now understood why Dalia had worn it.

"This is my cousin, Miriam Perelman," Dalia said. The lawyer's eyes jumped to Miri, taking in her harem pants and high-top sneakers.

"Nice to meet you, Miriam," he murmured. They all sat.

"So, Rocky..." Dalia began. "You and I haven't met before over personal business. But as I explained on the phone, Miri and I disagree with our cousin Seth's decision to sell the drawing. And rather than go out and hire a lawyer to stop the sale, I thought we'd try to settle this in conference."

"Sure. But I have to point out that Seth is not here."

Dalia waved her hand. "This is just preliminary," she said, prettily.

Silverman grunted. His warmth towards Dalia had evaporated. The flirting was over; he was all business.

"Go ahead, shoot," he said. "Whatcha' got?"

Dalia cleared her throat. "I don't think Seth *can* sell the drawing. I don't believe he has legal ownership."

Silverman's eyebrows went up. "He stole it?"

"I didn't say that. It's not clear who owns it."

"Hmm," Silverman said. "He told me he found it on a job site. His boss owns the house and said he could have it. That's fine. I know how to lean on the boss, if he changes his mind."

Miri blinked.

"But did he tell you that our great aunt sold the house to Seth's boss?" Dalia went on. "And that the contract said she still owned certain furnishings that had belonged to her family?"

Silverman made a low growling noise. "He told me the previous owner was upset over the disposal of an item that she failed to remove in a timely way. But he said she didn't appear to know or care about this drawing. Your great aunt, you say? He didn't mention that, no. Not that it matters. I don't care who she is."

"Well, she's already filed a lawsuit over the antique sewing machine," Dalia said.

"Are you threatening to tell the old woman about this drawing?" Silverman appeared to see Dalia in a new light. "So, you're looking to get yourself cut in on this? If that's the case, we really can't continue this conference any further."

Dalia sighed. "No, I didn't say I was going to tell her. Not yet, anyway."

Silverman made a face. "Listen. I have a client who's interested. If the art proves to be an O'Keefe, he's gonna have it, because I'm gonna get it for him. No bosses or old ladies, no matter whose great-aunt she is, are gonna get in the way."

Miri's heart had started to pound. Silverman thought he could win by force, but he didn't seem to know much about dealing with the art world. She was going to have to say something.

"I don't think it's going to be as easy as you...," Dalia began, but Miri cut her off.

"So, have you given it to an assessor yet?" she asked. She willed herself to be calm, but that had no effect on the butterflies in her stomach.

Silverman switched his eyes from Dalia to her. "I'm about to."

"I suppose it's Marc Rodriguez?" she said. Her voice sounded a little thin, but at least it wasn't shaking.

"How'd you know that?"

"I saw the Ellen Volotny litho you have out there." Miri nodded towards the outer room. "Marc Rodriguez works for Master's Gallery. They represent Volotny."

Silverman nodded. "OK, yeah, Rodriguez. Very clever."

"If he does the assessment on the O'Keeffe drawing, his work is going to be questioned because of what he did with that Goya sketch." Silverman seemed to puff up like a balloon. A balloon with a scowling face.

"I don't know what gossip you've listened to, but Marc made a mistake. That's all there was to it—a mistake."

For a second, Miri had begun to panic at his threatening scowl. But while young men like Seth or her ex-boyfriend Chuck could scare her, Silverman reminded her more of her father. Her father never got violent. He controlled her just by standing firm; nothing she said ever changed his mind. However, she had things to say to Silverman that would change *his* mind.

She gave him the side-eye. "He'd have to be pretty stupid to make a mistake like that, and he isn't stupid. I've met him."

Silverman shrugged and turned back to Dalia.

But Miri was just getting started.

"Did Seth tell you I have pictures of it?" she asked. She pulled her phone out of her pocket and quickly scrolled to the photos she'd taken that first day that Seth turned up at the restaurant.

"Give me that," Silverman said, holding out his hand. "I'm gonna have to delete those to protect my client. This needs to be kept quiet until he's ready to sell."

Miri slipped her phone back into her pants pocket.

"Too late," she said. Now she wasn't just calm, she was super-calm. "I've already sent them to three assessors and anyway, I've got these backed up."

The scowling balloon puffed up again, bigger this time.

"Who?" he demanded.

"One at the Georgia O'Keeffe Museum in New Mexico, one at the Smithsonian Institute, and one at the National Gallery of Art in Washington, D.C.," she told Silverman.

Silverman's eyes shot a death ray at her. His face worked as he thought over what she'd said. Finally, it settled into a sneer. "Well, thank you, little lady. That will raise the value of the piece nicely. I understand no new works by O'Keeffe have been found in years. The experts will be climbing all over each other to make the first offer."

He'd walked right into the trap, and she hadn't even finished setting it!

"No, the experts will be demanding to examine it in case this is another O'Keeffe fraud like The Canyon Suite mess," she said coolly.

Silverman froze…except, perhaps, for the twitch of an eyelid.

It was Dalia who asked. "Canyon Suite? You mentioned that last week. Explain."

"In 2000," Miri began, "an antiques dealer in Texas claimed she had discovered twenty-eight early watercolors by O'Keeffe. They came to her from her grandfather after he died. Her grandfather had known O'Keeffe; some people thought he'd had an affair with her. An art dealer bought the watercolors from the grand-daughter for a million dollars and named them 'The Canyon Suite' because O'Keeffe supposedly painted them in the town of Canyon, Texas.

She'd had a job teaching there. The Canyon Suite paintings toured some of the biggest art galleries in the United States: New York, Washington, D.C., Chicago, Philadelphia. Thousands of people paid to see them. It took the specialists six years to figure out that she *couldn't* have painted them."

"Why couldn't she?" Dalia asked.

"For one thing, some were painted on the wrong kind of paper—brands of paper that didn't even exist at the time that O'Keeffe lived in Canyon. In the end, the antiques dealer admitted they'd all been painted by other people, not O'Keeffe. She said she'd claimed they were O'Keeffe's just for the fun of it."

Dalia's eyes were open wide. "Are you saying this drawing could be a fraud?"

"*I* don't think it is, but you'd need a very reliable analyst to say that it's authentic. No...my point is that it's very risky. When you eventually put it on the market, every modern art specialist in the world is going to be all over you. The press is going to be all over you."

Silverman looked like he'd tasted a bad wine.

"Are you a modern art specialist?" he asked in a tone that was both soft and furious.

"Not yet," she said shortly.

"Why don't you just give us the drawing, Rocky?" Dalia said. "I don't think this is the kind of deal your client wants to get into. There's going to be a ton of publicity, and your expert is not reliable. Sounds like trouble to me."

Silverman stood.

"No way. She admitted she's no expert. That's a good story about the fraud, but she could be making it all up." His eyes were as stony as the eyes of the statue behind him. "Anyway, if Marc can't do it for some stupid reason, there are other art assessors. I'm not giving it to you or anyone until I know more."

He pushed a switch under the edge of his desktop. "Roddy," he said.

The young receptionist opened one of the double doors and leaned against the door jam. He was much taller and broader than he'd appeared to be when he was sitting behind his desk. He opened his lips and some metalwork on his teeth glinted.

"The meeting is over," Silverman said. "Get them out. I mean, *show* them out." He turned away in his chair.

Roddy stepped into the room and put a heavy hand on Miri's shoulder. She flinched.

"You were brilliant!" Dalia said, as soon as they turned the corner in front of the antiques store. You really know your stuff!"

"Some of it was lies," Miri said.

"*What?*"

"I do have backup copies of those photos, but I haven't sent them to the three experts."

"Huh. What about The Canyon Suite story?"

"Oh, that's true."

"Well, I think that's what got to The Rock. I've never seen him so upset."

"Yeah, but we didn't get the drawing back," Miri said glumly. "He's probably just going to take it to a different assessor." That's what she would have done. If she were in Silverman's shoes, she wouldn't give up on it, either. No one would, once they'd seen it.

Before she went to bed, she sent off identical emails with pictures of the O'Keeffe drawing to the Georgia

O'Keeffe Museum, the Smithsonian, and the National Gallery of Art. She was now fully committed to the legitimate art world.

Chapter 15

October 1918

It was close to midnight. Two dim electric lights caused weird shadows to play on the sheets that hung around each bed of the makeshift hospital ward. Sol had to sit outside the cloth enclosure where Ilka lay, his nose and mouth covered with a gauze mask. The darkness amplified sounds—raspy breathing, coughs, moans, the whispering of the nurses attending the dying, the shuffle of the orderlies' feet as they carried away another body on a stretcher.

New York had not been touched by the first wave of Spanish flu the previous spring. But in September, the influenza flared up again in a much more deadly form. Now it was rampaging through the city. Eight hundred people a day were dying, and they died fast, sometimes within hours of the first symptoms.

Sol had not slept in almost two days. The evening before, he'd come home at ten o'clock from the small workshop he'd rented for his rug business. The apartment had been empty, the stove cold. A scribbled note said,

Yussel sick Henry Street House

The hair on Sol's scalp had crawled. He had feared for Ilka and himself in the flu epidemic, but for some reason he had not expected it would strike Yussel. In a panic, he ran out to the street. Then, collecting himself, he set off for the Henry Street Settlement House.

Henry Street House had been started by Lillian Wald, a German Jewish woman from a wealthy family who had studied nursing and dedicated her life to caring for the poor, especially children. Ilka had taken classes there in childbirth and baby care when she was pregnant. So of course whenever Yussel was sick, that was where she brought him.

At first, Sol couldn't find her.

"I think…um, yes, she took him to the temporary ward around the corner," the night receptionist said. She would not meet Sol's eyes.

"What time did she bring our son in?"

The receptionist consulted a list. "One-fifteen this afternoon."

Nine hours ago! "Why didn't she send for me?"

"She fell ill." Sol's stomach tightened.

"Where is she?"

They're both in the temporary wards," the receptionist said reluctantly. "Your son is in the children's ward. Your wife is with the adults."

"How is…how is my son?"

"I'm sorry, I don't know." Once again, she looked somewhere else, not at him. "It's only a few doors from here," she said, pointing.

He ran.

ooo

Before going to Yussel, he stood briefly at the opening in the sheets around Ilka's cot. Sick as she was, half-conscious, she saw him. An imploring look flashed in her eyes: *save him.*

Yussel's cot was at the end of a row, near a stairway. The nurse did not put up much resistance when Sol demanded to sit by his child. Yussel lay, eyes closed, breathing with difficulty. At first, Sol murmured his love and memories to his son. But there was never the slightest response. So for the last hours, he simply held Yussel's fevered hand. The end came just after three a.m. That small, bright life had gone out, leaving the landscape of Sol's heart grey and dead.

Jewish law required that a body never be left alone from the moment of death until burial. Sol knew that Ilka would be deeply distressed if he did not follow that commandment. An orderly had gone to the office to telephone for the rabbi. So Sol closed the sheet around Yussel. Taking the pillow from his son's cot, he carried his child's body to Ilka's cubicle in the other room and laid him on the floor.

"Only until the rabbi comes with someone to take him," he told the nurse in this room. The synagogue had people who sat with the body when a family could not. And he could not leave Ilka.

He sat, thoughts wandering between past and present, eyes steady on Ilka's inert form, for the rest of the night. Would he lose her, too?

He'd agreed to marry Ilka at a point when he had lost faith in his dreams. Then, he'd been too proud to back out during their year-and-a-half-long engagement. After they were married, though, he'd lived up to his responsibilities. He thought he'd been a passably good husband; nothing to be ashamed of. But it was not the passionate romance he'd dreamed of.

When Ilka got pregnant, he'd felt unsure at first. *Children come, that's life*, he remembered thinking. But that was the last doubt about the baby that he recalled. Ilka had been so happy when she was expecting, so full of energy. It was impossible to be gloomy. And the moment the midwife put his newborn son into his arms, Sol was overwhelmed with love.

Yussel. He pulled his hair and rocked with the pain of loss. But he could not give way, could not let himself collapse into tears. Not yet.

When Rabbi Grinstein came, he wanted to pray with Sol, but Sol balked.

"God has just allowed my son to die," he said, barely keeping his emotions under control. "I will talk to him when I know if my wife will live or die."

"Then let us pray that she lives," the rabbi urged.

Sol was tempted, if only because he knew Ilka would have prayed for him. But he still resisted the old-world religion of the bearded rabbis who had schooled him. To him, those prayers only looked backwards.

"I have questioned God's actions too often to beg for a favor now," he said curtly.

Rabbi Grinstein looked shocked and started to argue.

"You pray," Sol told him. "Please," he added.

ooo

From the moment he'd first told her about it, even before Yussel was born, Ilka had loved the idea of making braided rugs from cutting room scraps. She had done a lot to make his idea a reality. She'd raised the startup money at the synagogue, enough for the workshop rent and the three sewing machines he now had, by talking enthusiastically to people she knew in the congregation.

After a few months, Sol had signed a contract with a medium-sized hotel—twenty-five rooms, fifty-two oval bedside rugs. Part of the agreement was permission to leave a few business cards in the desk drawer of each room. That had been Ilka's idea. *Durable enough for commercial use, handsome enough for your home,* the cards said. Ilka's English teacher at Henry Street House helped her get the words right. Sol hadn't thought much of the idea at the time, but Ilka had insisted. She'd nagged. When he finally asked the hotel owner for permission, the man said, "Oh, sure thing, Mr. Lefkowitz," one businessman to another. So Ilka had been right about that.

She had a head for business, no doubt about that. He would listen to her more. If she lived.

ooo

Ilka moaned and moved restlessly in the cot. Instantly, Sol was alert. Was this a turn for the worse? He stood and waved the nurse over when he saw her come out of a cubicle down the row.

"She's moaning. Is she worse?"

"I'll check. Stay there."

She whisked into the cubicle and twitched the sheets closed. Sol heard mumbling, the creak of the cot's wooden frame. After what seemed like an extremely long time, the nurse emerged carrying a bedpan.

"Her pulse is more normal and her fever is down a degree," she whispered. "But she's still in danger. If her temperature goes back up, it will mean that pneumonia is setting in."

"What can I do?"

"Find me if there is any change. I told her you're here."

"Did you tell her….?"

"No." She opened the corner of the sheet-curtain. "Watch her from here. Don't go in, Mr. Lefkowitz. Protect yourself."

Sol sat.

When for a moment the background sounds of coughing and moaning died down, he heard Ilka shift in her narrow cot.

"Sol?" she said softly.

In a flash, he was by her side. His pulse beat in his throat, half from hope, half from fear.

"No…don't come near. I just want to know you're there."

"I'll always be here for you, Ilka," he whispered hoarsely. "I love you. Please…get better. Live. Please, live."

Ilka must have heard in his voice what he couldn't tell her. She put her hand over her heart. Her face crumpled.

"He died?"

Sol bit his lip so hard he tasted blood.

"All of a sudden, he was so sick," she said, choking. "His lungs….

"Shh, shh."

"*Oh!*" she cried out, as if she'd been stabbed.

Sol took her free hand and enfolded it in both of his as his tears began. There was nothing he could say to ease the pain, but somehow they must share it. They must lean together and hold each other up.

Chapter 16
2009

The next morning, Miri was in the back office of the gallery, hunched over Bret's laptop. Dimly, she heard a customer come into the gallery from the street. Voices. Fast footsteps. The office door slammed open; a hand came down on her shoulder.

Roddy??

She screamed.

The hand spun the office chair around. Not Roddy. Seth.

A mixture of emotions passed over his face: he looked shocked and sorry at her scream, but then his eyes hardened.

"Sorry," he said shortly. "But I'm pissed. You went to see Silverman behind my back. You've mucked up my deal. You had no right to do that!"

Miri gathered herself. "You went behind *our* backs! You came to me—to Dalia and me—about the drawing! Then you gave it Silverman! Do you really think that creep is going to give you a cut of whatever his criminal client pays him for it?"

"He and I had an arrangement!"

"You had a delusion! Can't you see...."

Bret appeared in the doorway behind Seth.

"What's going on? Who is this?"

Miri froze. What if Seth blurted out something about finding a drawing by Georgia O'Keeffe? Bret would demand to see it.

"Family business," she muttered.

Seth looked offended. "Family business? It's *my* business! You think, just because you work in a gallery...."

Bret looked interested. "This has something to do with art?"

"This...it's all a big fantasy!" Miri said, desperately.

"You weren't calling it a fantasy last weekend!" Seth's voice was angry; but was there a note of desperation underneath the anger?

Miri's internal alarms were buzzing. If he even mentioned O'Keeffe's name, Bret would muscle in and take over. He'd fire her for not telling him she had an undiscovered O'Keeffe. He'd take full credit for finding it. She couldn't think of anything to stop him.

"Seth!" She stood, trying to give him a meaningful look, a look that said, *shut up!*

Seth's eyes flashed.

Mercifully, it was Bret who ended the moment.

"Hey!" he said forcefully. "This is not a bar. Take your business out of my gallery. That way, both of you!" He shooed them out the back door onto the small loading dock.

As she passed through the doorway, Miri fished her phone out of her pocket and speed-dialed Dalia.

"Seth is here. He's super-pissed."

"He is? That's great!" Dalia said. "Rock-o must have decided to change course."

Miri glanced at Seth. He stood on the other side of the loading dock, arms crossed, glaring at her. He looked angry, all right, but he also looked…What was that look? Resigned? She wasn't sure.

"So now what?" she asked.

Dalia thought. "You two grab a cab," she said. "Meet me at the northeast corner of Madison Square Park. Tell Seth I have a solution and it's to his advantage to listen. Wait…give him the phone. I'll tell him. And don't say another word to him about the drawing until we meet."

Neither Miri nor Seth broke the silence during the tense ride downtown. Miri stared out the window. When they arrived, Seth still looked upset. Miri felt ready to talk, if Seth would listen.

The walls of skyscrapers on all four sides of the two-acre park dwarfed the park's tall trees, and the buildings and trees dwarfed the park's collection of people. Benches held sleeping homeless men, agitated people waiting for a dealer, and black or brown-skinned nannies with white children. Old people fed squirrels, people in business clothes fast-legged the diagonal walkway, and two young men in California clothes stood in the center of the sidewalk waving their arms and pointing here and there—camera operators planning a shot, Miri guessed. She spotted Dalia on the fifth bench from the corner. Predictably, Dalia was making faces at a little girl whose mother was talking on her phone. She sighed and shrugged at the girl when Miri and Seth stood in front of her.

"Been waiting long?" Miri asked, sliding onto the bench on Dalia's left.

"Two minutes. Hello, Seth. Have a seat." Dalia patted the empty area of bench on her right.

Seth ignored her invitation. He stood, legs apart, arms crossed, facing Miri and Dalia.

"Did Rocky cancel your deal?" Dalia asked.

"You had no right to butt in—" Seth began.

"We had important information for him," said Dalia. "Which we are about to tell you. But first, please answer my question."

Seth scowled, weighing his options. Then, surprisingly, he decided in Dalia's favor.

"Not exactly," he said. "He talked about 'potential for fraud' and said the process was going to cost a lot more."

"Oh, I see," Dalia said. She glanced at Miri. "I guess you were right. He's going to look for another assessor. You need to tell Seth what you told Rocky. Both parts."

Miri explained about Silverman's connection with Marc Rodriguez and Rodriguez's shady past. "I had no idea he might be working with Rodriguez until we walked in there," she added.

"OK, that's why it might cost more. What's the potential for fraud?"

Miri swallowed and described the Canyon Suite "joke" that had fooled the art experts.

Seth sat down in the middle of the story, but when she reached the end, he stood up, looking angry all over again. "You *knew* all this, and you didn't tell me?"

"I…should have told you. I meant to when you came to my apartment. I mentioned it. You walked out just when I got to it. But you're right, I should have told you. I'm sorry."

Seth stared into her eyes for a long moment. Then he nodded. He walked in a circle, combing his fingers through his beard.

"But that Canyon Suite business doesn't mean this one is a fake," he said, half to himself. "There's something about it, something you can see, something I can feel."

Miri warmed towards him.

"Well, if you can feel its power, why do you want to sell it to some criminal who will just hide it away again? Art is meant to speak!"

Seth sighed deeply. "I need the dough."

Dalia spoke up again. "So what was your deal with Rocky? What did he offer you?"

"Twenty percent of the sale price," Seth said, grudgingly. "Within a month," he added pointedly.

"*Twenty percent?*" Dalia said. "When you could have had seventy percent, in the deal we proposed? Why would you go for that?"

"Within a month," Seth repeated. "No messing around with 'experts.'"

Dalia shook her head, as if to clear her thoughts. "Tell me—why don't you want to work with the professionals that Miri recommends?

"They're Establishment people." Seth's tone rose in pitch. "Always trying to make choices for me, push me into a life I don't want."

The frustration in his voice reminded Miri of what he had said on Saturday when she and Dalia visited his apartment in Battle Hill. She knew whom Seth was really angry with, whom he really meant by "Establishment people."

"Maybe your dad tries to push you in a direction you don't want to go," she said, keeping her voice quiet. "Professionals just give you options."

Seth's chin went down and his eyebrows pulled together as he took that in.

"You have it backwards, cousin!" Dalia said. "I wouldn't trust a word that gangster-lawyer says."

Miri spoke. "Like I said before: *you* came to *me*. Pursued me. Demanded my help. Now you want to toss out everything I offered and give it to a member of the *criminal* Establishment? A lawyer who gets rich keeping real criminals out of jail? That's just…stupid!"

Seth looked at the ground, his mouth a straight line. His bare, pointed chin quivered absurdly. Then his shoulders slumped, and he sighed again.

"That's true," he said reluctantly. "When you told me how much you thought it was worth, it totally blew my mind. It would have solved all my problems. I could have quit this shitty job, I could have really set myself up…."

"I thought something similar," Dalia said softly.

"So did I," Miri said.

The other two looked at her, eyebrows raised.

"Yeah," she admitted. "I did. It would be great to not have to take my father's help. To stand on my own."

One corner of Seth's mouth turned up. Standing and facing Miri and Dalia, he put one hand into the pocket of his jeans. "So we're all in the same boat," he said. "Problem now is, Silverman has the drawing."

Dalia took a deep breath. "You know what? Legally, I think the drawing belongs to Great Aunt Rina, same as the sewing machine. She was born in that house and she's owned it since her parents died. She only just sold it. We should have told her about the drawing first thing. Also, I think Rina might know some things about that piece of art that we don't know. We need to talk with her, right now. Do you want to come, Seth?"

Chapter 17
April 1920

Mickey the Kid was late to work. Sol stood in Mickey's place at the cutter's table, slicing wool fabric into strips to be braided into rugs. Any minute now, a shipment of fabric scraps from Sorkin's Suits would arrive downstairs and Sol would have to hurry down to pay the driver, then lug the bundles of cloth up four flights of stairs. When you owned the business, you had to do everything. In all his dreams of how his life would go, he'd never imagined anything even close to this. Counting Mickey, Sol's little business supported five employees plus himself, Ilka, and their new daughter, Ruth. It amazed him.

He glanced at the small alarm clock that ticked on his desk in the corner of the loft. Ten minutes to eight—Mickey was twenty minutes late! Sol put down his cutting tool and walked around the sewing table to Mrs. Tarnovsky. He'd already noticed that she was not her cheerful, gossipy self this morning. She kept her eyes on the rug she was stitching.

"Mrs. T, do you know if Mickey is sick today?"

Mrs. Tarnovsky's lower lip trembled. She had recommended Mickey for the cutter job when he and his mother, new immigrants, had moved into the apartment next to hers, and Mickey had proved to be first-rate. Back in

Kyiv, he'd been an apprentice at a textile factory, so he needed very little training. Although he was only eighteen, he'd already known the trick of flipping layers of fabric into order that Moishe Pinsky had taught Sol.

"Oy! I'm sorry, Mr. Lefkowitz," she said in a low voice. "I never meant to bring you trouble! Things are not right there."

"What do you mean, 'not right'?" Sol asked.

Mrs. Tarnovsky stopped sewing and wrung her hands. "It's his mother. Since they moved in, she was always quiet. I'd say 'hello,' sometimes she wouldn't answer. I thought she's not quite all here yet. But I had no idea! Last night, such a wailing and screaming from their apartment! It was terrible! I can't tell you the awful things I heard." She touched her temple and lowered her voice even more. "She's got a demon, poor thing, and last night it possessed her." She shivered. "She's lucky to be alive this morning."

"You're saying she has a mental illness?"

Mrs. Tarnovsky gave him the side-eye. "Call it what you like," she said. "I think it's the devil."

Sol closed his eyes for a moment. Mickey was struggling to support a sick mother. It would be harder for Sol to fire him, now that he knew. Not that firing employees was ever easy. Every time he had to fire someone, it brought back the feelings he'd had when Mendel fired him. Only, now, he was in Mendel's position. He had to choose between a business he'd created and a person who needed a job.

Just then, the buzzer from the delivery dock sounded. Sol clicked off the electric cutter and raced down four flights of stairs, glad to have a task that would take his mind off Mickey.

But on his six slower trips back upstairs with bundles of cloth on his back, he had time to think. He pictured

Mickey's bright blue, shoe-button eyes, his red-blond hair that never lay flat, his gawky arms and legs. The kid was always in motion, full of energy.

After a stop at the front entrance of the building to collect the day's mail, he climbed the four flights for the last time. Upstairs, Mickey had arrived.

"Sorry, boss. My mother is sick and I had to find someone to stay with her." Mickey spoke with breezy confidence, but his eyes were troubled.

"And you found someone?"

"A neighbor."

"A responsible person?" Sol persisted.

Mickey's confident mask almost slipped. His glance darted towards Mrs. Tarnovsky. Sol read his fear that she had told him about Mrs. Margolin. Mickey mutely nodded.

"Good, good," Sol said and squeezed Mickey's shoulder.

Returning to his battered desk in the corner, he busied himself opening envelopes. One of the letters contained an inquiry from a furniture store in Brooklyn! Despite this good news, he brooded over the situation with Mickey.

It bothered him that so many people, like Mrs. T., thought that mental illness was caused by the devil. He believed what modern science showed — that mental illness had a cause and that it could be cured. Whenever he had a chance, he went to the public library and read psychiatric journals. They were full of articles about trauma from the Great War, which had just ended.

Later, when Sol was bringing his ledger up to date, he noticed an unusual quiet in the workshop. He had dimly noticed Mickey leaving to go down to the toilet on the third floor. But Mickey had not returned and Mrs. Tarnovsky's seat was vacant as well.

He found them on the stairs.

They both looked up guiltily when Sol opened the door to the stairwell.

"What's wrong?" Sol asked.

Mrs. Tarnovsky raised her hands and let them drop. She gave an exasperated sigh. "It's not right!"

"It's not your business," Mickey said.

"There I don't agree," she answered. "What you did to your mother is *not right!* I don't care what demon she has in her head."

"*Zey shtil, yente!*" Mickey said. *Be still, you busybody!*

"Mickey," Sol said, "what happened to your mother?"

"Ahh! She's OK, Mr. Lefkowitz. She has spells sometimes, that's all."

"I see. But what is Mrs. Tarnovsky upset about?"

"I'll tell you!" Mrs. Tarnovsky burst out. "I asked him who is watching her? And he says the old Italian woman from the apartment downstairs. I said, that woman couldn't stop a turtle, much less a wild woman. And he tells me it's fine, because *he tied his mother to a chair!*"

"Last time she told me to!" Mickey burst out. "She said, 'If this happens again, just tie me down!' You think I like to do it? But if I lose my job, how will we eat?"

But Mrs. Tarnovsky clearly had more news to spill. "I heard her last night—until two-thirty in the morning, she was yelling!" Her voice whined upward into a cat-like howl that echoed in the empty stairwell. "'I want to die,' she was yelling. 'Let me die!'"

A chill ran down Sol's spine.

"Mrs. T.," he said. "Let me talk to Mickey in private."

Mrs. Tarnovsky's eyes flicked nervously from Sol to Mickey. Frozen-faced, she climbed three steps and passed through the door.

Mickey was sniffling and making little gasps as he wiped his eyes and nose on his sleeve.

Out of nowhere, Sol suddenly recalled old Rabbi Yehudah back in Volnavoda, instructing him that soothing bruised souls was a great *mitzvah*. But he hardly knew where to begin. He patted his pockets, but he didn't have a handkerchief.

"You're a good worker, Mickey," he finally said. "You wouldn't be easy to replace. It would hurt my business and it would hurt me to fire you."

Mickey's blue eyes widened with hope.

"But I need someone who's here every day. The business is so small, there's no one to cover for you."

Mickey's head dipped.

"Also, tying up someone who's in a crisis is…" Sol wanted to say 'cruel,' but thought better of it, "…not the modern treatment," he finished, although that wasn't true. Just about every mental institution used straightjackets.

"She wasn't this way before the pogrom," Mickey said hoarsely. "It's what they did to her…."

Sol had lost track of how many armies had overrun Kyiv—Germans, Poles, the White Russian Army. There had been terrible pogroms against the Jewish population only the year before, in 1919.

Sol shook his head. "I'm very sorry for what she suffered. I would like to try to help her. If you want me to."

Mickey squinted at Sol, assessing him, and Sol suddenly saw himself as Mickey saw him: thirty years old (old!); well fed; dressed in an expensively cut blazer jacket (bought for almost nothing because the pockets had been sewn in backwards); and most importantly, wearing the invisible mantle of authority.

"Don't send her to an asylum," Mickey blurted. "You can't lock her up. Her spells only last a day or two. The rest of the time, she's OK. Not like before, not happy, but OK. Only, if you put her in an asylum...."

"I would like to find a doctor to treat her."

"A doctor? But I have no money."

"I understand. Maybe I can find a way. I can try."

Lefko Rugs now made enough profit that Sol had a small cushion against disaster in the bank. He knew he shouldn't risk that, but starting the business had taught him something about how the world worked. It had shown him how life involved exchanges. Hadn't Izzy said something like that once? When you could, you gave a little and that balanced what life took away from you. In his life, little Yussel had already been taken from him. Of course, salvaging the lives of Mickey and his mother couldn't even begin to balance that loss — nothing could. Still, he would do what he could.

ooo

On Friday afternoon, when his shop was closed for the Jewish sabbath, Sol went uptown to the campus of Columbia University to find Dr. Ernst Steinberg, author of an article on treating soldiers with war trauma. Sol had read the article in the public library. It described exactly the kind of symptoms that Mickey's mother had — occasional flashbacks, terrors, and loss of the sense of reality. Sol hoped the professor would advise him on how to help her. Perhaps he would agree to treat her himself.

Sol was able to describe Mrs. Margolin's symptoms and to give Mickey's explanation of the cause — what the soldiers had done to her. Steinberg listened closely, his hands resting on the blotter pad that covered his desk, his eyes focused somewhere near Sol's face but not exactly on it. At the end, however, he looked down at his hands and sighed.

"If you brought me a soldier, or any man with those symptoms, I could help. But for this woman, Mrs. Margolin is it?— I don't know anyone who could provide psychiatric care," he said slowly. "Here's the problem, you see. Psychiatric treatment is given through talking. It would have to be someone who spoke her language. And her trauma is a woman's trauma. We have no female psychiatrists. I've heard there are a few in Europe, but none in the United States. Would she talk to a man about this?"

Sol struggled with disappointment. "Where else could I go to find help for her?"

"Possibly someone in the nursing school or the public health department would have a better answer than I do. I'm very sorry."

ooo

"It didn't go well?" Ilka asked taking one look at Sol's face.

She picked up the baby and bounced her gently as she listened to Sol's story.

"Nursing school," she murmured. "You know, I was thinking when you told me about Mrs. Margolin.... Of course, a doctor would be better, but I have seen women like that at Henry Street House."

"What do you mean?"

"Scared. Nervous. Women with troubles. I talked to one of them. She was new from Fastov in Poland. The pogrom there...ach! I could see she was still shaking inside."

"And they treat her at Henry Street?"

"There is a nurse there—maybe she's from England? Her English is different. I heard she is trained in this psychiatry."

"From England. Does she speak Russian or Ukrainian?"

"I don't know. But she speaks Yiddish."

Sol thought for a long moment.

"We do the best we can." he said finally. He kissed Baby Ruth and put his arm around Ilka. "We do the best we can, and we hope the best will come of it."

Sunday, June 16, 1932

Finally, they were leaving the little house on Marsh Street where they had lived for twelve years, since Sol had brought his braided rug business to Battle Hill from the Lower East Side of New York City.

Every day the radio news reported the suffering caused by the Great Depression. People had lost their homes; families were living in tents. But thanks to a contract with Gimbels Department Store in New York City and then with Gimbels in other cities, business was good for the Lefko rug factory. Sol and Ilka had saved, and finally they were able to build a bigger house in Battle Hill.

Ilka tore off a piece of paper tape, wet the glue side with a sponge, and smoothed it across the top of the ninth carton of books. There! The bookcases were empty. She sighed and stretched, one hand pressed to the small of her back.

Rina, age seven, lay sprawled on her stomach on the braided rug that covered the living room floor. Her feet waved above her like the antennae of an art-seeking ant.

Tongue poking between her lips, she was copying the abstract charcoal drawing that usually hung on the side of a bookcase next to the desk in the corner. Normally it was hidden from most of the room, but Rina had taken it down and propped it up in front of her, against the bottom drawer of the desk.

"Rina, darling, can you get up? I need to walk around and you're in my way."

"I'm making a present for Papa!" While her mother had spoken in Yiddish as always, Rina answered in English.

Ilka glanced down at her youngest daughter's work. As usual, Rina's hand was surprisingly sure, her eye sharp.

But as to the subject of her drawing… Ilka's mouth stretched into a thin line. She had always struggled with her feelings about that picture. Eventually, Sol had confessed that he'd told a lie—told it within minutes of their marriage! The woman who gave them the picture wasn't his boss's daughter; she was his ex-girlfriend. He'd met her on a tourist boat, the way American couples met, rather than by an arranged match. Ilka imagined that they'd been immediately attracted to each other. She'd imagined this many times. Sol said he kept the picture because of the art itself, not because it reminded him of *her*. (Ilka knew the ex-girlfriend's name: Rose.) She remembered the moment that woman had walked uninvited into their wedding reception wearing the most elegant afternoon gown that Ilka had ever seen. A brief silence had fallen; everyone had stared. Sol said Rose had made him believe he would find his place in America, but he'd come to understand that he and she were too different to share that place. Ilka thought there was more to the story.

She sighed. Jealousy was like a chronic infection. It kept coming back.

"So sit at the desk where I won't step on you," she said, bending down and sweeping up a handful of the crayons scattered on the rug. She was about to stuff them into the box, when a loud "*Brrring!*" shredded the air.

They both froze.

Dropping the crayons, Ilka straightened up slowly, wiping her hands on her skirt. Rina turned interested eyes on her mother.

"Telephone, Mama," she said, tipping her head towards the device, which sat on the desk.

"*Brrring!*"

"May it grow a boil in its throat," Ilka muttered. This Yiddish curse did not surprise Rina. All three children were very aware of their mother's dread of the telephone. She panicked when she had to speak English rapidly into that cold metal device. "Ruthie! Come and answer, please," Ilka called.

Rina looked expectantly through the kitchen, in the direction of the bedroom that she shared with her sister and brother. Two nights before, when they were in their beds, Ruth had declared that she wasn't going to handle the next call. "Sink or swim," Ruth had said. "If she has to do it, she will."

"*Brrring!*"

Rina scrambled to her feet. "Can I answer? I can do it!" Rina's friends either didn't have telephones in their homes or weren't allowed to use them. Rina longed for a chance to hear a voice that came through a wire.

"No." Ilka took a deep breath. She marched to the desk, picked up the telephone, and snatched the earpiece from its hook. "*Allo?*" she said, too loudly. Rina winced.

"What is your business with him?" Ilka half-shouted in English. She paused. "OK. Just a minute. I'll get him."

She set the phone and receiver down on the desk with relief and sailed through the kitchen to the back hall. The ceiling hatch was open and the steps leading up to the attic were unfolded.

"Sol!" she called. "Someone is calling you by the telephone! Aron…Aron Teitelbaum."

Sol came down the steps. Ilka followed him towards the living room.

"Now, you won't forget today is Father's Day," she said.

"I won't forget."

"Because the children are excited."

"I know."

"And I'm making a nice dinner."

"I smell it. Brisket?"

"No. An American dish. *Pot roast.*"

Sol turned and smiled at her. "Such a fuss!" he said.

Ilka bit her lip. She still wasn't used to the gap in his smile where he'd had a tooth pulled just the month before. And how long had he had that crease next to his eyebrow?

"Hello?" Sol said, taking up the telephone.

While he spoke, Ilka again picked up crayons and silently urged Rina to take her sketch pad outdoors.

"Yes, all right," Sol was saying into the telephone. "In half an hour, then." He hung the receiver on the hook.

"Are you going to the office, Papa?" Rina asked.

"Just for a short time."

"But it's Father's Day!"

"I know, little one, but someone needs my help."

"When will you be back?"

"As soon as I can. I won't be long."

"That's what you said last time!" Ruth said from the kitchen doorway. Sam was just behind her.

"Ruth," Ilka rebuked her. "We'll wait for you. We'll have dinner when you're back,"

The three children all looked down, hearing in her remark that Sol would be gone for the rest of the afternoon.

"Oh, I'll be back in an hour. I've already talked to Aron once. We just have to make a few arrangements."

Ilka put her hands on her hips. "If you're not here by five o'clock, Sol, I'm going to call you at your office!"

Sol chuckled. "Oh, now you're giving me a reason to stay longer, just to make you do that." He kissed her and left the house.

"I don't get it," Rina said. "Why does someone need Papa's help today, anyway?"

"One of his workers probably has a wife who went bananas," Ruth said.

"Bananas? What are you talking about?"

Ruth made an awful face, with her tongue hanging out of one side of her mouth, and circled her finger in the air next to one ear.

"She means mentally ill," Sam put in.

"Oh," Rina said. "What is Papa going to do?"

"He's going to send the person to a psychiatrist," Sam said.

"And he's going to *pay* for the psychiatrist," Ruth added. "Why does he have to get involved with those people? Why doesn't he mind his own business? The kids at school...."

"The kids say something to you? About your father helping his workers?"

"Some of their fathers work for Papa," Ruth said.

"So?"

"They know families with crazy people go to him and he gives them money. Some of them say...." The corners of

Ruth's mouth pulled down and her lips began to tremble. "…Things."

Ilka was silent. She would have to talk to Sol about this. She knew, however, that Sol would not stop offering help to his employees. She reached her arm towards Ruth and gave her a hug.

"Listen to me, Ruth. Your father is a good man. He helps unfortunate people. And he's a *learned* man. He studies scientific books to understand these terrible problems. This was his calling in life; he wanted to study the mind since he was a boy. There was just no way he could get the education that he needed. But helping a few employees—that he can do."

She well remembered the first time Sol had gotten involved with an employee, when he'd helped Mickey Margolin's mother. Ilka herself had provided the solution that time, a nurse at Henry Street House back in the Lower East Side. Mickey had made the move to Battle Hill with his mother. Now he had a wife and children and he still worked for Sol.

"Hmph," Ruth said. "I bet the new house would have been finished a year ago and we'd be living there now if he wasn't giving so much money to those *unfortunate* people."

"Is your homework finished?" Ilka asked. "If you want to spend this evening with your papa, you'd better have it all done."

"It would go faster if I had my own room," Ruth shot back. She disappeared into the bedroom, slamming the door behind her.

Ilka shook her head.

"And you, my little girl," she said reaching out to Rina. "Come on, take your crayons and paper outside. The movers are coming in a week and I still have so much to do!"

Rina made a small noise of dissatisfaction, but flipped her sketchpad closed. She had finished copying the drawing. She trudged out the front door with her sketchpad and Crayola box.

When she was alone, Ilka stood thinking. Life constantly offered problems—some small, others larger. Her current problem was huge: uprooting the family from this overcrowded house and starting anew in a bigger, better space. It wasn't difficult, but there was a deadline, she was under pressure.

She found herself staring at the charcoal drawing that had hung in her living room since they'd moved to Battle Hill. It sat on the floor, propped up against a leg of the desk. The drawing was a small problem, one that bothered only her. With no clear intention in mind, she bent over and picked it up.

Hearing her mother climb the attic steps, Ruth quietly opened the bedroom door and peered out. Ilka was holding the drawing against her body with her left arm as she used her right hand to help her climb the shaky wooden stairway. Why was she taking it up to the attic? Ruth's forehead wrinkled at the baffling ways of adults, but she said nothing, then or ever.

Chapter 18
2009

"Dalia, dear!" Great Aunt Rina said the instant the three cousins walked into her small apartment. She held out one wrinkled arm. "Come sit by me."

Rina was eighty-four years old. Her back was bent and her head canted forward. But her cheeks were smooth and carefully made up with a rosy tint. Dalia dropped onto the couch and, right before Miri's eyes, transformed into the teenager she had been. She laid her head on Rina's shoulder. Rina drew her close.

Miri shifted her gaze to Seth. He was gazing at Rina, eyes wide open.

"Come in, you two," Rina said, beckoning Miri and Seth forward with her free arm.

"Oh!" Dalia sat up. "You remember Miri, and this is our cousin Seth, Ira's son."

"Seth!" Rina reached and Seth took her hand. "I wouldn't have recognized you. You don't look a bit like your dad."

Seth stood up straighter and smiled. "You knew him when he was my age?"

"Well, of course I did. I knew him from the time he was born. Ira was always headstrong. Why don't you turn that chair around and sit over there." Rina's voice was not loud but it resonated like an old bell.

Miri's eyes fell on Rina's walking cane, which leaned against the arm of the sofa. It was the type with a backward bend to the shaft and a horizontal hand grip that turned up at the front end. Rina had painted it to look like a colorful snake with its head reared back, about to strike. The snake's back was dark orange with yellow and red spots, and its belly was iridescent blue.

"Do you like it?" Rina asked, following Miri's eyes. "It's a Brazilian rainbow boa."

"Gorgeous. That must have been fun to do," Miri said.

"Well, yes, it was. But people's reactions to it are even more fun." Rina held her hand out to Miri and pulled her close for a quick kiss on the cheek. "So good to see you again, dear!"

Miri perched on a small, 1960's-style armchair, facing the others.

She could see that Seth's expression was hyper-alert and alive with changing emotions. Clearly, Rina was not what he had expected. She surprised Miri, too. The last time she'd met her great-aunt, Rina had merely seemed kind. This time, she seemed to hold a special power.

Rina turned back to Dalia, who had curled up again, nestled against her. "What's happened to you, Dalia, dear? You look wilted, like you need to be watered with love. You were always such a passionate child," she murmured into Dalia's ear.

Passionate child? Miri wondered about that. Dalia was a controlled, rational lawyer. *Except when she isn't,* she thought, remembering Dalia's confessions during their dinner together.

"Shh. That's a secret," Dalia said.

"Oh, nonsense. Your whole generation is bewitched by passion—to hear you talk, anyway. Isn't that your goal? To 'follow your passion?'"

Dalia sat up and puffed out a surprised breath as if she'd been touched in a sensitive spot.

"Yes, that's what we want," she said. There was a bitter note in her voice. Miri felt the sting of Rina's remark too. She had followed her passion—and what had it gotten her besides frustration, debt, and pressure from her father?

Rina ignored their reaction. "Every generation wants the same thing," she said. She paused and thought for a moment. "…in America, anyway. We thought *we* were going to seize our passion in life. We thought *we'd* get so much farther than our immigrant parents ever could."

"Well, you did, didn't you?" Seth put in. "It was easier for you. You grew up here. You didn't have to figure it all out."

Miri was still absorbing the change in Seth's attitude—how he'd taken to Rina. *He was so suspicious of Dalia and me,* she thought. And then she thought, *Wait. No. We were suspicious of him.*

Rina snorted. "We had the Great Depression to figure out, dear. And after that, there was the Second World War. We had our dreams, but in the end most of us did what we had to do to survive. We stuck with our families. We grew up watching our parents struggle, helping them when we could; we couldn't walk away from them. Or at least, I couldn't. It's all different for you, isn't it? You have to depend on your parents to get a toe-hold."

Seth scowled.

Miri sympathized.

"Speaking of toe-holds, where are you living and what are you doing to put bread on the table?" Rina asked Seth.

"I'm a carpenter here in Battle Hill. I took a demo job as a start, to get some local experience. Well, actually, I took what I could find...."

"Well, that explains the muscles and suntan," Rina said. "You look much too healthy to be in law school, following your dad's example."

Seth stretched his legs forward and tipped the dining room chair back. He ran his fingers through his curly mop of hair.

"That's what *he* wanted me to do, all right," he said with force. "But it's not for me. Sitting in front of a computer and twisting the law for my clients? That's not my kind of life. I need physical work!"

"I see. It sounds like you know yourself. Very wise. The world needs carpenters. Are you in the union?"

"No. Well, I'm doing rough carpentry now, but what I really want to do is design and build furniture."

Rina smiled. "I wanted to be a painter," she said. "There is an artistic streak in our family. I suspect it bypassed Ira."

Seth snorted and rolled his eyes. But he looked pleased, Miri decided.

Dalia sat up, suddenly businesslike.

"Actually, speaking of art, we came to show you something, Rina," Dalia said. "Wait 'til you hear where Seth is working. Seth, tell her the address of the house you're tearing down."

"I guess it's where you once lived," Seth said. "Thirty-two Marsh Street."

Rina sighed. "Well, I knew it would come down when I sold it. Ironic that it's you, my own relative, doing it. How did that happen?"

Seth shrugged. "By chance. It was in pretty bad shape inside," he added, as if that would soften the emotional blow.

"But there was one thing inside it," Dalia said, nodding at Miri. Miri brought up the photo of the drawing on her phone and passed it to Rina.

"Is this about my step-gran's sewing machine?" Rina asked, fumbling for her glasses.

"Oh…no. This is in addition to that," Dalia said.

Having shoved her glasses into place, Rina took Miri's phone, looked at the photo, and froze. After a long moment, she pushed her head closer and stared some more. Slowly, the hand holding the phone sank to her lap. Tears stood in her eyes.

"It must be sixty-five years since I've seen this," she whispered. "Oh! This brings back…" She didn't finish the thought. "It's a Georgia O'Keeffe, isn't it?"

"Yes." Miri exchanged a look of shared knowledge with Rina. "At least, that was my feeling the moment I saw it. We still need an expert opinion, though."

"So different from her oil paintings," Rina said. "I must have been in college when I first saw some of O'Keeffe's drawings. I thought of this immediately." She raised the phone. "But as far as I know, it was lost when we moved from Marsh Street. You have it? Where is it?"

"Seth found it.," Dalia said. "It was in the attic of the Marsh Street house."

"In the *attic*? All these years? How can that be?"

"I found it behind the boards. It looked like someone had placed it there pretty carefully," Seth said. "There must have been some insulation there once. Later, it seems, a layer of fiberglass was installed over the boards."

"Behind the boards," said Rina. "Placed there carefully. Do you mean hidden?" She looked bewildered. "Who would have done that?"

"That's what we'd like to find out. We were hoping you would know," Dalia said.

"I don't have the slightest idea."

"But can you identify it? Can you show that it actually belonged to your family?"

"That we owned it?" Rina blinked. "I don't know. It was a wedding gift to my parents, I believe. So they didn't buy it. There wouldn't be a receipt. But we had it in our house—in the Marsh Street house."

"When was the last time you saw it?" Dalia asked.

"Well…I seem to remember that my mother was packing for our move…. Yes! Come to think of it, yes, I do have proof—of a sort. Come with me. You tell me if it's good enough."

Using her cane, she pushed herself to her feet. She snatched up a bunch of keys from a small table and pulled open the door of her apartment. "Come along. This way." When they were all out in the hall, she locked the door and set off toward the elevators at a surprisingly fast pace.

"Where are we going?" Seth asked.

"To my storage area, downstairs. You'll see."

They all entered the elevator car. When the door slid open again, they were facing a hallway. Bare lightbulbs in the ceiling lit unpainted wooden walls. To the left, the rumble of washing machines and dryers came from a lighted doorway. To the right, more doorways without doors led into dark spaces. Dalia, in the lead, turned in at the second opening and switched on the light.

Locked cubicles made of wire fencing lined the walls of the room and a sturdy wood table stood in the center. Rina fumbled with her keys in front of one of the cubicles. Finding the key she wanted, she was about to push it into the padlock. But instead, she half-turned around.

"Where is it now, though? You haven't told me yet."

Miri and Dalia exchanged glances. Miri looked over at Seth. His eyes flashed. He licked his lips.

"I didn't know it was yours," he said. "I didn't know you lived in that house once. My boss didn't want it and I thought I'd sell it."

Rina took this in.

"It's *sold*?"

"Not yet. No. We want to get it back."

"I see." She looked relieved. "From a gallery? Or an art dealer?"

"From a crooked lawyer," Dalia said.

Rina's eyebrows wrinkled. She looked around at the three of them, waiting for an explanation.

Dalia cleared her throat. "We all have reasons to want money," she said. "Quick money. Although…" She glanced at Miri, giving her credit, "Miri tried to convince us to go the long route and sell it the right way."

Rina turned fully around and leaned on her cane.

"You were going through a crooked lawyer who was going to sell it the *wrong* way?"

There was a silence.

Miri felt the blood rushing to her cheeks. She couldn't look at Dalia or Seth. Yes, she too had wanted easy money, just like them. She remembered Rocky Silverman throwing them out of his office and her stomach tightened.

Leaning on her cane, Rina turned her head from side to side, raking the cousins with her sharp brown eyes.

"Quick money? I don't know what your money problems are, but I'm sure the way to solve them isn't through a crooked lawyer," Rina said. "But you said you didn't know it was mine. You didn't know it it was—it *is*—part of the legacy of your family."

Miri peeked at Rina. Under the yellow light bulb, the old woman's face appeared mottled with strong emotion and at the same time, fragile.

Seth's eyes were stricken.

"It was my dear father's," Rina went on, "and I'm the only one of his children left. You should have come to tell me about it before you tried to sell it. Well, at least you're here now. So, here's what we're going to do. We're going to get it back. All of us. Together."

"But how?" said Seth.

Rina held up a finger, turned, and unlocked the cubicle door.

"First, the proof you asked for. Come here, Seth. Just a couple of weeks ago I was going through that box there. Can you put it on that table, please?"

He did as she asked. The box was labeled "Sol's home files." The cellophane tape had been sliced so the flaps opened easily. Rina rapidly pulled out file folders, checked the contents, and piled them on the table.

The fifth folder apparently held what she was searching for.

"It's surprising, the things sentimental parents keep," she said. She pulled out a large envelope. It was addressed in a neat but childish hand to *Papa*.

Inside was a folded, yellowed, piece of heavy paper that might have come from a sketch pad. As Rina unfolded it, Miri sucked in a breath. Across the top was printed, "Dear Papa, Happy Father's Day. Your daughter Rina. June 16,

1932." Underneath was a close-to-accurate copy of the Georgia O'Keeffe drawing. All the shapes were in their correct positions. The copy even captured the feeling of movement in the original, although the rising ovals had been changed to look like flower buds.

Chapter 19

September 1945

Sol knocked on his son's bedroom door.

"Yes?" Sam said from within.

"Your mother wants me to ask you something before you get dressed."

Sam opened the door. "What's up?" he asked, gesturing Sol into the room.

As he turned the desk chair around and sat down, Sol heard the doorbell chime downstairs. The dinner guests had arrived. Someone else would have to let them in.

His eyes rested warmly on his twenty-four-year-old son, who sat on the side of his narrow, childhood bed. Sam's hair was still damp from his shower. He was wearing his old plaid flannel bathrobe, which had been hanging in the closet for three years. His feet were bare because his slippers had disappeared while he was gone and Sol's slippers were too small for Sam's big American feet.

Sol wanted to touch those feet. He wanted to put his hand on his son's hair, just beginning to grow out of the Army haircut he'd worn when he arrived home three weeks before. Sol was skeptical about miracles, but "miracle" was the only word he could think of to describe the fact that Sam had been returned to them, alive and whole, after three years in the army, the last nine months fighting the *Wermacht* and Mussolini's army in Sicily.

This dinner was a small celebration of Sam's homecoming.

"What does she want?" Sam prompted. "Why didn't she come ask me herself?"

Sol gestured at Sam. "You're not dressed and she's up to her elbows, cooking. She would like you to wear your uniform for dinner."

A series of emotions crossed Sam's face, ending in regret. His head dipped.

"I can't, Pa." He massaged his forehead. "I just can't put that thing on." Sol saw tears gathering beneath his son's eyelashes, not for the first time since Sam had come home. This was concerning. He'd tried to convince Ilka to go easy on Sam, not to press him to do anything. But she wanted to admire her wonderful son, the army corporal, decked out in his battle ribbons.

The doorbell chimed again.

"Don't worry about it," Sol said soothingly. "She wants to say she's proud of you, that's all. We both are. But whatever you wear will be fine. It's *you* we're happy to have back. The dinner is about you, not the uniform."

Sol heard quick steps on the flagstone floor of the entryway, below: his daughter, Rina, was answering the door. Dimly, he heard Izzy greeting her and Rina inviting Izzy and his wife in.

Sam had tented his hands over his eyes. He muttered something.

"What's that?"

"I don't deserve a party for surviving," Sam said, and began to cry.

It was as Sol had suspected, but worse. He'd seen this kind of reaction after The Great War, twenty years before. Back then they called it shell shock. Now there were new names. Sam had been trying to hide it, but Sol had seen the sudden tears and twice had seen him suppress a panic attack. He mentally scolded himself for not facing the problem before this. It hurt to see trouble in people he loved.

He leaned forward and put his hand on Sam's shoulder.

"Now I understand," he said. "Your mother and I wanted to celebrate, but maybe it's too soon for you. We should have realized."

Sam struggled to control his sobs.

Sol moved to the bed and pulled Sam into a hug. At this, Sam broke down entirely. He clung to Sol, rolling his head from side to side in some kind of a "no," but unable to form words.

After a minute or two, Sol spoke into Sam's hair. "I never talked about it, but back in Russia the pogroms came through my town. I was just a teenager. It happened twice. Who lived and who died—it made no sense. What happened, happened. Good people, bad people—nobody deserved what they got. And surviving didn't mean you had it easy, either."

Sam's body stilled. He raised his head and looked up with reddened eyes. "I was the one with the gun," he said.

"I know," Sol said gently. "In a war, both sides have guns." He squeezed Sam's shoulder. "It will get better. It takes time."

Sam shook his head again. "It's not right that it should get better," he said thickly.

"It's not fair to the dead that it should get better, but yes, it's right," Sol said. "You have life. To *not* live it—that would be wrong." He gently moved away from Sam and stood. "Come. Splash some cold water on your face." He helped Sam stand and guided him into the hall towards the bathroom. "Forget about the uniform. Come downstairs when you're ready."

Sam hugged him before going into the bathroom.

ooo

An opening in the wall of the second-floor hallway looked down on the entryway. The area below—the *foyer*, the architect had called it—was now empty. The sun slanting in through the beveled glass panes next to the door caused a rainbow to glow on the plaster wall. That rainbow in the afternoons always lifted Sol's heart with a sense of peace. He paused there to give himself time for his emotions to subside.

He had surprised himself by remembering the terror of the pogroms in Poland. He hadn't thought of that in years. And his judgment—that moving on with life was morally right, although it might not be fair to those who had senselessly died—could have come straight from old Rabbi Yehudah at Sol's yeshiva in Volnavoda. He shook his head. He thought he'd come a long, long way from the ancient, mystical attitude of the old rabbis. And yet, here were their very words, coming out of his mouth.

His daughter Rina's laughter came from downstairs, sweetening his thoughts. Stepping lightly, he went down the stairs and across the hall into the living room.

Two logs were burning in the Spanish-style fireplace. Rina sat in the armchair to its right. Her new boyfriend, Irving, was balanced on the arm of her chair, kissing her.

Sol shook his head, smiling. Here was the difference between America today and the world that he'd grown up in. By the standards of America in 1945, a kiss in her parents' living room wasn't daring at all. Still, Sol had to admit it made him a little uncomfortable.

Next to the door, bottles of liquor and a bucket of ice were set out on a table. With his back to Rina and Irving, Sol dropped ice cubes into a glass and made himself a whiskey and soda—a small splash of whiskey and a lot of seltzer water. He didn't want to get tipsy.

When he turned around, Irving was standing next to Rina's chair.

"Good evening, Irving," Sol said. "Glad you could make it." Irving had driven up from the Bronx that afternoon. Sol liked the young man, although he was surprised that Rina had chosen him. Since she'd started in the art program at the University of Pennsylvania, she'd only dated other art students. Irving was in the business school there.

"Evening, sir," Irving said.

Sol waved away the "sir."

"Rina, did I hear Izzy and Bernice at the door?"

"Yes, they're saying hello to Mama."

"And someone called on the phone?"

"It was Uncle Mendel. They'll be a little late. They were just leaving."

"Mmp!" Sol said. Hanna and Mendel were almost always late. "I'll go and get Izzy and Bernice out of your mama's hair."

Ilka was sure to be in the near-frenzy stage of producing a dinner party, a stage well known to her family. But with visitors in the kitchen, she would contain her urge to fly around the room like a demented bat. The effort was hard on her, he knew, and it would be a shame if anything went wrong with the food. He headed down the hall and turned into the kitchen.

ooo

"Heyyy, Nebbish!" Izzy cried. He slapped Sol on the shoulder and they hugged.

"Good to see you!" Sol said. "Bernice, you look beautiful." Bernice was as tall as Izzy and still slim. Even wrapped in a large brown apron, she was elegant. Normally, he would have hugged her, but she was chopping an onion with a long chef's knife. Tears ran down her face, making channels in her face powder.

Sol winced. "A lot of crying today," he said.

Ilka, bent over the open oven door, looked up from basting the roast.

"Who's crying?" she asked.

"Sam's not going to wear his uniform at dinner," he told her. "I think the war was harder on him than he wants us to know."

Ilka straightened up. "He *cried*?" She frowned. "Something hasn't been right with him since he got home. "I thought maybe if we celebrated, applauded him…. What was I thinking? Going to war is not like taking a trigonometry test."

"Don't worry, he's OK. Let's forget the uniform, though."

Ilka pushed the roast back into the oven and snapped the door closed.

"You're sure?"

"Yes, sure. He'll be down soon."

Ilka sighed. "Bernice, let's have those onions in the skillet."

Sol turned to Izzy, who was leaning against the counter next to the refrigerator. Izzy's body was relaxed but his eyes glinted with attention. Izzy and Bernice's son, Joe, who was five years younger than Sam and only a private, was still stuck in Europe waiting his turn for a ship home. Sam's safe return had been reassuring to them and they had been delighted to be invited to the celebration.

"Let's get out of the way here," Sol said. "Come and have a drink." He jerked his head towards the hall.

Izzy looked around quickly and grabbed a lemon out of a basket on the counter before following Sol.

Back in the living room, Irving was bent over the back of Rina's chair, telling her a story. Izzy improvised a rum sour while Sol refreshed his whiskey and soda.

"I guess Sicily was pretty bad?" Izzy asked quietly.

"Mmm. He'll be all right." Sol didn't want to worry Izzy. "How was California?" he asked. Izzy and Bernice had just returned from a vacation out West.

"Gorgeous. Bernice fell in love with L.A." Izzy sipped his drink while sizing up Sol's composure. Then he dropped the bomb. "We ran into your old girlfriend there."

"*What?!*" The word came out louder than Sol intended. Rina glanced over. "Who are you talking about?" he added, more quietly.

"Who do you think? Rose. We were walking downtown and we passed a big building under construction. The sign said 'Koestlic Designs.' Well, I knew that name…and there she was, in slacks and a hard hat, walking around with a roll of blueprints in her arms telling all the men what to do."

After a long moment, Sol forced himself to inhale.

"Designs…?" he said.

Izzy nodded. "She's an architect with her own firm. Doing quite well."

He pulled out his billfold and plucked a card from it. "Rose Koestlic, F.A.I.A.," it said.

"I went over and said hello," Izzy went on. "We had a nice chat. After she got her degree from Barnard, she moved to California. Designed a lot of buildings out there. The whole state is under construction."

Sol shook his head in wonder. "She did exactly what she said she would do."

"Why not? If you have enough money, you can do whatever you want," Izzy said dryly.

"*Hm!*" For a crazy moment he imagined himself alongside Rose as she climbed the steps of her career. Then he let the image go. He would have been a dead weight on her. And without Ilka's support and his children to spur him on, his own life would have come to nothing.

"Did she ask about me?"

Izzy laughed at him. "What do you think, Nebbish? She remembered *me* right away. You think she forgot *you*?"

Sol saw Rina look over at them. He put his hand on Izzy's sleeve to get him to lower his voice. But he couldn't leave the subject.

"What did she say? What did you tell her?"

"I told her you were looking at the waste bin one day, got an idea for making braided rugs, and now you lived in a big house in Westchester County."

Sol burst out laughing. "So *that's* the last twenty-five years of my life?"

"Who are you talking about, Papa?" Rina interrupted.

Sol frowned and waved the subject away.

"A ghost from your dad's past," Izzy said wickedly.

"Izzy," Sol warned.

"Ghost?" Rina asked. "You said *her*. Who was she?"

Sol rolled his eyes at Izzy. "No one," he said. "Just someone we used to know."

But Izzy wasn't letting him off. "*No one?* Of all the young women who were throwing themselves at his feet, he only noticed two. She was the first. That's who."

Sol snorted. "Women throwing themselves at me? Why didn't I notice that?"

"You see other people, but you don't look in the mirror," Izzy said.

"What happened with her?" Rina asked, intrigued.

Sol shrugged. "Eh, she wasn't really interested. Probably married some wealthy guy."

"As a matter of fact, she never married," Izzy put in. "Too busy, she said. Probably a rich guy would have bored her."

"Enough, Izzy," Sol said. "You're making a mountain out of an ant hill."

"Mole hill, Poppa. It's 'making a mountain out of a mole hill.'" Rina corrected him, as he knew she would.

"OK, mole hill," Sol said.

Suddenly everyone noticed Sam standing just inside the living room doorway. Had he just appeared, or had he been there for a while? He was dressed in an old plaid sport shirt tucked into a pair of his old trousers. Izzy, who was nearest the door, stepped close to him.

"Sammy!" he said, quietly. "Good to see you! We're glad you're home."

He held out his hand.

"I'm sure Joe will make it back soon, too," Sam said, as they shook.

Izzy lowered his face to hide his feelings. "He'd better!" he said. He patted Sam's shoulder. "My generation left Europe to escape hate and violence. I'm sorry we had to send our sons back across the ocean to fight the same enemy. It's a terrible thing that so many died."

Sol involuntarily extended his fingers towards his son, but Sam did not crumple. Instead, he blinked, and his gaze shifted to the distance, taking in this larger view.

"This is not the life I expected your generation to have," Sol told him.

"What did you expect?"

"That you would be free, I guess, free of the immigrant life. That you would live like any American, free to do whatever you chose." *Like Rose,* he thought. "Instead, you had to go back to Europe and fight the Fascists--an even more horrible aggression than I had to deal with."

Sam pressed his lips together but said nothing.

Izzy quirked an eyebrow. "It's better for him here, though," he said. "He knows his way around. Don't forget: he grew up here."

"There's still prejudice," Sol objected. "And Sam is still considered part of our community—not equal, no matter how bravely he fought."

"Oh, now," Izzy objected. "Maybe it's slower than you thought it would be, but there's still progress."

Sol couldn't picture it. "Will Sam's children live an American life?" he wondered aloud. And then, to himself, he thought, what about the next generation? What about his great-grandchildren? "If only we could see the future," he murmured.

Izzy rolled his eyes and sighed. "If only," he said.

Chapter 20
2009

Back upstairs, Rina sank into an armchair.

"We'll go see this lawyer, the one Dalia says is crooked," she promised the three cousins. "Just as soon as I get my energy back together. Dalia, dear, would you switch on the electric kettle? I need a cup of tea. Do any of you want some tea? No? There's some 7-Up in the fridge."

"I'll get it," Miri said.

Rina settled herself in the chair.

"Seth," she said, "why did you give the drawing to this crooked lawyer?"

Seth looked uncomfortable.

"It was my fault," Dalia Jumped in. "Seth picked up on something I said. At that point, I didn't realize he was working at your old house. I had no idea you might have any connection to it. I...went off the tracks."

"Oh?" said Rina?

"Yes. I...brought up selling it on the black market. I know this criminal defense lawyer...."

But Seth broke in impatiently. "You said we were all going to go get it back," he said to Rina. "All of us together. How?"

"We're going to march into his office and demand what's right," Rina said.

"Dalia and I tried that," Miri said. "It didn't work."

"Then we'll try it again. When you know something is wrong, you have to resist."

"Maybe you have to believe resisting will make a difference," Seth said. Miri agreed with him but she said nothing. Dalia only sighed.

"Of course it makes a difference! Let me tell you something. I grew up in a union family. My father, your great-grandfather, marched in the Uprising of the Twenty-Thousand, back in 1909."

"Uprising of the Twenty Thousand! What's that? I never heard of it."

"Well, you should have. Maybe they don't teach about it out in Seattle, but it's part of American history. He was so proud of it."

"They didn't teach us about that in St. Louis, either," Miri said, pouring soda into glasses. "What was it?"

"Hmph," Rina said. "The Uprising of the Twenty-Thousand was an enormous strike, one of the first really big strikes in the garment industry in New York City. More than half of the workers were Russian Jewish immigrants, like our family."

Miri felt mild surprise. She rarely remembered that their family had been immigrants three generations ago.

"The women led the strike because they were exploited the most," Rina went on. "They were out on the street for two months in the freezing winter, marching, getting badly beaten up by thugs the management hired. The strike fund ran out, there was no money to buy food. It was hard. But they won, mostly, and it was a big turning point for all unions."

"But our great-grandfather was a factory owner," Miri said. "Why would he be marching for the union?"

"I heard he was an A-1 guy," Seth put in. "Rich. "

"Mom always said he was a big businessman," Dalia said.

Rina drew back her chin.

"He wasn't always a factory owner. He was an ordinary worker for years. He sewed men's suits, and he was a cutter. But then he had an idea and started a little carpet business on the side, at night. It was seven or eight years before he got a big contract and the business began to take off."

"He had an idea and it turned into a factory. Huh," said Seth. "I never heard how he got started." He was silent for a few seconds. "But all that stuff about unions and fighting the good fight, following your dream and striking it rich…. That doesn't work anymore. That's not the world we live in now."

"Well, it never did happen to many people," Rina said. "Of course, back before the Great Depression it was easier because the economy was in overdrive. People were trying all sorts of things to make money. Most of them failed. To succeed you had to have a good product, but you needed some luck, too. My mother was part of my father's luck—she helped him in a lot of ways."

She cocked her head at Seth.

"You said the world is different now. How is it different?"

Seth frowned at the question.

"We don't know what's really happening," he said slowly. "Everything's connected by computers and the internet. We don't know who's controlling things. There's no simple path to get to your goal anymore. We're screwed from the beginning."

"Well, that's a theory," Rina said dismissively.

Miri raised her eyebrows. She understood perfectly what Seth meant.

"In your generation," Rina went on, "everyone expects to be a tremendous success with a million 'followers.' The people my father knew all lived in a few square blocks of New York. All they wanted was to survive, put food on the table and get along in life. Of course, they dreamed big—why not? The dreams kept them going. And some of them did succeed—like your great-grandfather. They didn't always find the success they were looking for, but they did what they could."

"I wish I'd known him—my great-grandfather," Seth said. "I'd like to build something of my own." He sounded wistful. "Something useful and beautiful."

Miri smiled. Was this the guy who'd trusted no one, who'd seemed so crude, who'd had no use for art, only for money?

Rina was nodding. "He would have liked you," she said. Then she gave him a searching look and spoke gently. "But why *did* you give the drawing to that lawyer in the first place?"

"I've had some problems," Seth said. "I'm trying to make a new start and I need money. Miri wanted to get it analyzed by experts, but I need the money now."

"Hm." Rina nodded. Miri could not have called her reaction sympathetic, but it wasn't critical, either. "Well, that drawing means a lot to me. It's part of our family history. I've never forgotten it. I'm grateful to you all for finding it. I owe you a lot for that."

ooo

The cab pulled up in front of Rocky Silverman's office building. The driver got out and tried to help Great-Aunt Rina get out of the back seat, but Rina was having none of that. She pushed his hand away and used her snake-painted cane to pull herself to standing upright in the street. She and the three cousins gathered on the sidewalk in front of the building. A couple of passersby gave her cane the side-eye and steered clear.

When they entered, Roddy the receptionist stood.

"Whoa!" he ordered.

Rina poked the snake-head end of her cane into his chest. Roddy froze, wide-eyed. Stepping around Rina, Dalia opened the door to Silverman's office as Roddy glared helplessly. At the last moment, Rina removed her cane and followed the other three into the inner office.

"What's this?!" Silverman exclaimed, standing up.

"You've got my O'Keeffe drawing," Rina snapped, stepping to the front of the group. "I can prove it's mine and I want it back right now."

Silverman looked from her to Dalia with narrowed eyes.

"This your great-aunt?" he asked. "So you told her I had it. Why am I surprised?" He turned to Rina. "You sold the house, Madam. What you didn't take doesn't belong to you anymore."

"Wrong," Rina said. "The contract allows me to remove items of sentimental value. That drawing was my father's. It's very important to me. You'll give it to me now or I'll have you in court so fast your head will spin. And more than that, I'll talk to every reporter I can get my hands on and put this mess in front of the whole country. I'm positive it's an O'Keeffe, so it will be a very big story. How will your client like that?"

Roddy stepped into the office, looking scared.

"Sorry, Uncle Rocky. She put a freeze-spell on me with that staff. You want them out?"

Silverman ignored him. Instead, he turned to Seth.

"You told me it was yours. My client is a violent man. He doesn't like to be lied to. I don't like it, either."

"And you believed his story without checking it out?" Dalia said coolly. "That wasn't very careful, Rocky."

"I didn't know about her then," Seth said. "I didn't know it used to be her house."

"I will not let you have it," Rina said to Silverman.

"The situation has changed, Rocky," Dalia said. "My great-aunt is prepared to sue you for the drawing. As she says, it will make a big splash in the media."

"And have you forgotten that I wrote to three museums about it?" Miri put in. "The experts are going to demand to see it any second now."

Miri heard, in her own voice, a confident, new tone. She was finally one hundred percent on the right side of this whole business—the side of the legitimate galleries and museums. Briefly, she wondered where the drawing would end up, if Silverman gave it to them. On some private buyer's wall? No. It should be in a museum, where anyone could see it.

Silverman's face and neck slowly darkened with the effort of suppressing his anger. He stared past Miri as he weighed the situation. She forced herself to keep her eyes on his face, displaying confidence, she hoped. In the silence, she could hear her own pulse throbbing in her ears.

At the end of his calculations, Silverman pushed his chair back a few inches and fiddled with something at the level of his knees in his desk. Miri heard the loud click of a lock releasing. He brought out the O'Keeffe drawing. The layers of bubble wrap that she had applied three days earlier had been pulled apart and loosely rewrapped. He tossed the bundle towards the group.

"Get out!" he snarled.

Seth managed to catch it. His eyes darted around as if he were playing the children's game of hot potato and he desperately needed to pass it to someone. Miri opened her arms to receive it.

The drawing was still in its frame, unharmed. Relief flooded through her. They had saved it. She cradled it as she took a deep breath and felt her future open before her. She would get a worthy job… Her dad would finally respect the life she'd chosen...

"Uncle?" Miri heard Roddy ask softly as Rina and the three cousins filed out of Silverman's office.

"You have to know when to cut your losses," Silverman snarled.

Just before Rina reached the door to the street, she suddenly stopped and wheeled around. "For your information," she called, "we're taking this straight to my bank and putting it in my safe deposit box. So don't bother sending anyone to my rooms."

There was no reply.

After stopping at Rina's bank, they went back to her apartment.

Miri felt a growing tension in her body. When they walked into Rocky Silverman's office, the four of them were equal partners on a mission to recover the drawing. But now that it was in Rina's safe-deposit box, their great-aunt was in control. What stake did the three cousins now have in the drawing?

"You know, in some way, that drawing was part of my father's success," Rina began. "He loved it, he kept it near him. He said it gave him hope that all his struggles in life were going to work out. And they did work out for the most part. It's not easy to change cultures and languages as an adult, but he made a success of it."

"If he loved the drawing so much, why'd he hide it in the attic?" Seth asked.

"I still can't believe he did that."

"Then how'd it get there?"

Rina threw up her hands. "I wish I knew!" She shook her head. "It's a complete mystery."

Miri couldn't stand the suspense any longer. "So, what are you going to do with it?" she blurted.

Rina sat back in her chair.

"In a roundabout way, all of you gave it back to me. I think we should all decide together. I have an idea, but I'd like to hear yours first."

There was a silence. The three cousins looked at each other. It was Seth who broke the silence.

"I think we should donate it to a museum, where everyone would be able to enjoy it."

Miri's mouth dropped open. She looked quickly at Dalia, who had sprawled on the couch. Dalia was nodding. "Way to go, Seth," she said.

Seth smiled.

"You really don't want the money?" Miri asked. "Why?"

Seth got up and walked to the kitchenette. He got the liter of 7-Up out of the fridge and unscrewed the cap. His eyelids were lowered, but Miri thought she caught a gleam in his eyes that reminded her of the little redheaded boy under the table at a wedding, so long ago.

"When I first found it, it was just a little thing that maybe I could sell. And when you told me how much it might be worth—wow. It totally blew my mind."

He poured soda into an empty glass.

"But you were right," he said to Miri. "Selling it on the black market was a bad idea. I knew Silverman was bad when I met him, but he was even worse than I thought." Seth shook his head. "He had the drawing right there in his safe the whole time he was telling me he'd already given it to that appraiser guy. But that's not the real reason I've changed my mind."

"What's the real reason then?" Miri asked.

"Well, you were part of why. I know I resisted, but…" He seemed to get stuck for a moment, then forced himself to go on. "It's good to be part of a family. My dad…is a bitter person. Alone. And he wanted me to be just like him, which I'm not. Being part of this family…"

He paused, then went on.

"Aunt Rina, what you were telling me about Great-Grandfather Solomon--like, that he was a working guy starting out, standing up to the bosses side by side with his fellow workers, fighting for a better deal—and then he started a business that turned into this big factory? Golly! And all along, it was this little drawing that helped him and inspired him? I mean—wow!

"When I found it, I had no idea it was connected to *me* in any way. But now that I know about the connection, I have to ask myself: what would *he* want me to do with it? Sol Because I feel like he's here with us right now. And what he would have wanted matters. Miri's right. Selling it for quick money means selling it to some bad person who would hide it away and then use it to dodge the law.

Solomon wouldn't want that. I guess he'd want other people to see it and be inspired by it, too. So that's how I vote."

"I second that," Dalia said.

"Third!" Miri said with enormous relief.

Rina nodded. "Well, then, we all agree, because that's what I want, too. I admit, if I were hurting for money, it might not be so easy for me. But...." She turned to Miri. "Tell me what you know about this: A friend of mine inherited a statue and she donated it to a museum. It had been in her family for three or four generations and it was too big for her little apartment. The museum couldn't pay her what they said it was worth, but they did pay her—more than a little—even though she offered it to them for nothing. Is that the way it works? Might there be a little something coming in return if we donate this? If there is, I'm happy to let you three split it. I don't need it."

"Maybe, maybe not," Miri said. "Depends on the museum. But yes, it *could* happen."

"I see," said Rina. "Well if it works out like that, I will make a gift of the money to each of you."

Dalia sat up straight.

"Would it be enough to pay my way to getting a teaching certificate?"

"You're going to quit your job?" Miri asked.

"I'm thinking about it," Dalia said. "I've wanted to for a long time, and now...now maybe I can. I wish we had the drawing here," she went on. "It's changing my life and I hardly got more than a peek at it."

Rina pulled herself out of her chair and crossed the room to her desk.

"I was only seven when I made this," she said, holding out her childish work. "It's a poor copy. But it will remind you."

Dalia took it. "I like touching it," she murmured. "It's like touching the past. It feels alive."

"Still alive..." Miri echoed. For a moment, she was lost in thought. "You know, when you and I visited the house on Marsh Street, Dalia, I looked around that space and I imagined a whole line of people---many people, many lives—going back to Great-Grandfather Solomon and beyond. Seth feels connected to him, and you feel like the past is still alive. But I wonder…what was his life really like? How did my life, my struggle, grow out of his? I can't picture it."

She sat still for a short time.

"But you know what? It's nice to have a family, don't you think? We should get together sometime, for dinner or something."

She looked around, from Seth to Dalia and back to Seth. His gaze was open and relaxed. Dalia's was turned inward and she was humming a little tune under her breath. Miri's eyes met Rina's, who was observing the three of them with a smile.

Sources

One of the sources for this book is a family story about my grandfather. According to my mother, he tried to work for a relative selling souvenir caps on a tourist boat on the Hudson River, but he was no good at it because he didn't have a salesman's personality. He was more of a scholar. In this country he eventually made his living buying, building, and selling houses and apartment buildings. On my mother's birth certificate, however, his profession is listed as "ragman"—a person who collects and deals in old clothes. To me this means that early on, he worked at whatever he could find to support his family.

When I have asked my cousins about grandfather failing at cap-selling, none of them had ever heard that story. We know so little of the lives of our forebears, and they, of course, had no way to imagine ours.

No other detail of Solomon Lefkowitz's life is based on my grandfather's. For example, he didn't immigrate to the Lower East Side of New York City, but to Albany. The bottom line is that ninety-nine percent of this novel is based on my imagination and research.

Research

Invaluable to picturing life in the Lower East Side of Manhattan in the 1900s was a live, virtual tour I took of the Tenement Museum at 97 Orchard Street, New York.

Among the books I read about the life of Jewish immigrants in New York City and Europe in the 1910's and earlier, I recommend Alfred Kazin's memoir *A Walker in the City*. Other books worth looking at include *The World of Our Fathers*, by Irving Howe; *The World of Our Mothers*, by Sidney Stahl Weinberg; and *How We Lived: A Documentary History of Immigrant Jews in America 1880-1930*, by Irving Howe and Kenneth Libo.

Most of my research, however, was conducted online. Some of the articles I read there can be found online at the following links (or at least could be when I finished writing this book.)

- Life in a Polish shtetl, including some photographs
  https://yivoencyclopedia.org/article.aspx/Shtetl
- Life in the Lower East Side of New York:
  https://www.loc.gov/teachers/classroommaterials/presentationsandactivities/presentations/immigration/polish6.html
- Revolution and unrest in Poland, 1905-1907:
  https://en.wikipedia.org/wiki/Revolution_in_the_Kingdom_of_Poland_(1905–1907)
- The Educational Alliance:
  https://socialwelfare.library.vcu.edu/settlement-houses/educational-alliance/

- Laundering money for stolen art:
  https://www.nytimes.com/2021/06/19/arts/design/
  money-laundering-art-market.html
- New York garment factories in 1910:
  https://eportfolios.macaulay.cuny.edu/karacas2017/2
  017/05/26/from-sweatshops-to-factories-the-history-
  of-the-new-york-city-garment-industry-stacy-shapiro/
- Railway lines in Europe, 1913:
  http://www.vidiani.com/maps/maps_of_europe/old_
  maps_of_europe/large_detailed_old_railway_and_stea
  mship_map_of_europe_1913.jpg
- IRT elevated & subway lines 1906:
  https://www.nycsubway.org/wiki/Historical_Maps#1
  900-1910
- Significance of Sabbath candles:
  https://www.learnreligions.com/what-do-candles-
  represent-in-judaism-2076656
- Uprising of the 20,000:
  https://en.wikipedia.org/wiki/New_York_shirtwaist_
  strike_of_1909 ;
  https://en.wikipedia.org/wiki/Clara_Lemlich
- Canyon Suite Forgery:
  https://www.nytimes.com/2000/03/07/arts/arts-in-
  america-if-it-s-not-an-o-keeffe-exactly-what-is-it.html
- Ashkenazi wedding customs:
  https://en.wikipedia.org/wiki/Jewish_wedding
- Psychiatric nursing.
  https://currentnursing.com/pn/introduction_to_psyc
  hiatric_nursing.html

Acknowledgments

First, I wish to thank the members of the several writing critique groups to which I have belonged, who gave me insightful comments at various stages of the book's development. In no particular order, these would include Erica Jolly, Tara Tanner, Janet Asbridge, Jennifer Lindsay, and Sharon Adelman Reyes.

I am also grateful for the support of my family concerning my writing, especially of my husband, Victor Dallons, who makes it possible in many ways for me to work, and of my sister, Deborah, always encouraging.

Finally, many thanks to Tamim Ansary, who did a wonderful job of editing, formatting, and publishing this book.